ILLUSTRATE
YOUR OWN

Fairy
Tales

ILLUSTRATE YOUR OWN

Fairy Tales

The History Press

First published 2020

The History Press
97 St George's Place, Cheltenham,
Gloucestershire, GL50 3QB
www.thehistorypress.co.uk

British Library Cataloguing in Publication Data.
A catalogue record for this book is available from the British Library.

ISBN 978 0 7509 9493 4
Typesetting and origination by The History Press
Printed in Turkey by IMAK

Contents

1

Sleeping Beauty

Once upon a time there lived a King and a Queen, who lacked but one thing on Earth to make them entirely happy. The King was young, handsome, and wealthy; the Queen had a nature as good and gentle as her face was beautiful; and they adored one another, having married for love – which among kings and queens is not always the rule. Moreover, they reigned over a kingdom at peace, and their people were devoted to them. What more, then, could they possibly want? Well, they wanted one thing very badly, and the lack of it grieved them more than words can tell. They had no child. Vows, pilgrimages, all ways were tried; yet for a long while nothing came of it all, and the poor Queen especially was in despair.

At last, however, to her own and her husband's inexpressible joy, she gave birth to a daughter. As soon as the palace guns announced this event, the whole nation went wild with delight. Flags waved everywhere, bells were set pealing until the steeples rocked, crowds tossed up their hats and cheered, while the soldiers presented arms, and even strangers meeting in the street fell upon each other's neck, exclaiming: 'Our Queen has a daughter! Yes, yes – Our Queen has a daughter! Long live the little Princess!'

A name had now to be found for the royal babe; and the King and Queen, after talking over some scores of names, at length decided to call her Aurora, which means The Dawn. The Dawn itself (thought they) was never more beautiful than this darling of theirs. The next business, of course, was to hold a christening. They agreed that it must be a magnificent one; and as a first step they invited all the Fairies they could find in the land to be godmothers to the Princess Aurora, that each one of them might bring her a gift, as was the custom with Fairies in those days, and so she might have all the perfections imaginable. After making long inquiries – for I should tell you that all this happened not so many hundred years ago, when Fairies were already growing somewhat scarce – they found seven. But this again pleased them, because seven is a lucky number.

After the ceremonies of the christening, while the trumpeters sounded their fanfares and the guns boomed out again from the great tower, all the company returned to the Royal Palace to find a great feast arrayed. Seats of honour had been set for the seven fairy godmothers, and before each was laid a dish of honour, with a dish-cover of solid gold, and beside the dish a spoon, a knife, and a fork, all of pure gold and all set with diamonds and rubies. But just as they were seating themselves at table, to the dismay of every one there appeared in the doorway an old crone, dressed in black and leaning on a crutched stick. Her chin and her hooked nose almost met together, like a pair of nut-crackers, for she had very few teeth remaining; but between them she growled to the guests in a terrible voice:

'I am the Fairy Uglyane! Pray where are your King's manners, that I have not been invited?'

She had in fact been overlooked; and this was not surprising, because she lived at the far end of the country, in

An old crone. dressed in black.

a lonely tower set around by the forest. For fifty years she had never come out of this tower, and every one believed her to be dead or enchanted. That, you must know, is the commonest way the Fairies have of ending: they lock themselves up in a tower or within a hollow oak, and are never seen again.

The King, though she chose to accuse his manners, was in fact the politest of men. He hurried to express his regrets, led her to table with his own hand, and ordered a dish to be set for her; but with the best will in the world he could not give her a dish-cover such as the others had, because seven only had been made for the seven invited Fairies. The old crone received his excuses very ungraciously, while accepting a seat. It was plain that she had taken deep offence. One of the younger Fairies, Hippolyta by name, who sat by, overheard her mumbling threats between her teeth; and fearing she might bestow some unlucky gift upon the little Princess, went as soon as she rose from table and hid herself close by the cradle, behind the tapestry, that she might have the last word and undo, so far as she could, what evil the Fairy Uglyane might have in her mind.

She had scarcely concealed herself before the other Fairies began to advance, one by one, to bestow their gifts on the Princess. The youngest promised her that she should be the most beautiful creature in the world; the next, that she should have the wit of an angel; the third, a marvellous grace in all her ways; the fourth, that she should dance to perfection; the fifth, that she should sing like a nightingale; the sixth, that she should play exquisitely on all instruments of music.

Now came the turn of the old Fairy Uglyane. Her head nodded with spite and old age together, as she bent over the cradle and shook her crutched staff above the head of the pretty babe, who slept on sweetly, too young and too innocent as yet to dream of any such thing as mischief in this world.

'This is my gift to you, Princess Aurora,' announced the hag, still in her creaking voice that shook as spitefully as her body. 'I promise that one day you shall pierce your hand with a spindle, and on that day you shall surely die!'

At these terrible words the poor Queen fell back fainting into her husband's arms. A trembling seized the whole Court; the ladies were in tears, and the younger lords and knights were calling out to seize and burn the wicked witch, when the young Fairy stepped forth from behind the tapestry, and passing by Uglyane, who stood scornful in the midst of this outcry, she thus addressed their Majesties:

'Take comfort, O King and Queen: your daughter shall not die thus. It is true, I have not the power wholly to undo what this elder sister of mine has done. The Princess must indeed pierce her hand with a spindle; but, instead of dying, she shall only fall into a deep slumber that shall last for many, many years, at the end of which a King's son shall come and awake her. Whenever this misfortune happens to your little Aurora, do not doubt that I, the Fairy Hippolyta, her godmother, shall get news of it and come at once to render what help I may.'

The King, while declaring himself infinitely obliged to the good Fairy Hippolyta, could not help feeling that hers was but cold comfort at the best. He gave orders to close the christening festivities at once, although the Fairy Uglyane, their spoil-joy, had already taken her departure; passing unharmed through the crowd of folk, every one of whom wished her ill, and riding away – it was generally agreed – upon a broomstick.

To satisfy the King's faithful subjects, however, – who were unaware of any misadventure – the palace fireworks were duly let off, with a grand set-piece wishing Long Life to the Princess Aurora! in all the colours of the rainbow. But His Majesty, after bowing from the balcony amid the banging of rockets and hissing of Catherine wheels, retired to a private room with his Chamberlain, and there, still amid the noise of explosions and cheering, drew up the first harsh proclamation of his reign. It forbade every one, on pain of death, to use a spindle in spinning or even to have a spindle in his house. Heralds took copies of this proclamation and marched through the land reading it, to the sound of trumpets, from every market-place: and it gravely puzzled and distressed all who listened, for their women folk prided themselves on their linen. Its fineness was a byword throughout the neighbouring kingdoms, and they knew themselves to be famous for it. 'But what sort of linen,' said they, 'would His Majesty have us spin without spindles?'

They had a great affection, however (as we have seen), for their monarch; and for fifteen or sixteen years all the spinning-wheels were silent throughout the land. The little Princess Aurora grew up without ever having seen one. But one day

– the King and Queen being absent at one of their country houses – she gave her governess the slip, and running at will through the palace and upstairs from one chamber to another, she came at length to a turret with a winding staircase, from the top of which a strange whirring sound attracted her and seemed to invite her to climb. As she mounted after the sound, on a sudden it ceased; but still she followed the stairs and came, at the very top, to an open door through which she looked in upon a small garret where sat an honest old woman alone, winding her distaff. The good soul had never, in sixteen years, heard of the King's prohibition against spindles; and this is just the sort of thing that happens in palaces.

'What are you doing, goody?' asked the Princess.

'I am spinning, pretty one,' answered the old woman, who did not know who she was.

'Spinning? What is that?'

'I wonder sometimes,' said the old woman, 'what the world is coming to, in these days!' And that, of course, was natural enough, and might occur to anybody after living so long as she had lived in a garret on the top of a tower. 'Spinning,' she said wisely, 'is spinning, or was; and, gentle or simple, no one is fit to keep house until she has learnt to spin.'

'But how pretty it is!' said the Princess. 'How do you do it? Give it to me and let me see if I can do so well.'

She had no sooner grasped the spindle – she was over-eager perhaps, or just a little bit clumsy, or maybe the fairy decree had so ordained it – than it pierced her hand and she dropped down in a swoon.

The old trot in a flurry ran to the head of the stairs and called for help. There was no bell rope, and, her voice being weak with age and her turret in the remotest corner of the palace, it was long before any one heard her in the servants' hall. The servants, too – in the absence of the King and Queen

She dropped down in a swoon.

– were playing cards, and
could not be interrupted
by anybody until their
game was finished.
Then they sat down
and discussed
whose business
it was to attend
on a call from
that particular
turret; and this
again proved to
be a nice point,
since nobody
could remember
having been
summoned thither,
and all were against
setting up a precedent (as
they called it). In the end they
decided to send up the lowest of the
junior page-boys. But he had a weakness
which he somehow forgot to mention – that of fainting at the
sight of blood. So when he reached the garret and fainted, the
old woman had to begin screaming over again.

This time they sent up a scullery maid; who, being good-
natured and unused to the ways of the palace, made the best
haste she could to the garret, whence presently she returned
with the terrible news. The servants, who had gone back to
their game, now dropped their cards and came running. All
the household, in fact, came pouring up the turret stairs;
the palace physicians themselves crowding in such numbers
that the poor Princess Aurora would have been hard put to

it for fresh air could fresh air have restored her. They dashed water on her face, unlaced her, slapped her hands, tickled the soles of her feet, burned feathers under her nose, rubbed her temples with Hungary-water. They held consultations over her, by twos and threes, and again in Grand Committee. But nothing would bring her to.

Meanwhile, a messenger had ridden off post-haste with the tidings, and while the doctors were still consulting and shaking their heads the King himself came galloping home to the palace. In the midst of his grief he bethought him of what the Fairies had foretold; and being persuaded that, since they had said it, this was fated to happen, he blamed no one but gave orders to carry the Princess to the finest apartment in the palace, and there lay her on a bed embroidered with gold and silver.

At sight of her, she was so lovely, you might well have supposed that some bright being of the skies had floated down to earth and there dropped asleep after her long journey. For her swoon had not taken away the warm tints of her complexion: her cheeks were like carnations, her lips like coral: and though her eyes were closed and the long lashes would not lift, her soft breathing told that she was not dead. The King commanded them all to leave her and let her sleep in peace until the hour of her awakening should arrive.

Now when the accident befell our Princess the good Fairy Hippolyta, who had saved her life, happened to be in the Kingdom of Mataquin, twelve thousand leagues away; but news of it was brought to her in an incredibly short space of time by a little dwarf who owned a pair of seven-league boots. (These were boots in which you could walk seven leagues at a single stride.) She set off at once to the help of her beloved goddaughter, and behold in an hour this good Fairy arrived at the palace, in a fiery chariot drawn by dragons.

Our King met her and handed her down from the chariot. She approved of all that he had done; but, greatly foreseeing as she was, she bethought her that, as all mortals perish within a hundred years or so, when the time came for the Princess to awake she would be distressed at finding herself orphaned and alone in this old castle.

So this is what she did. She touched with her wand everything and everybody in the palace: the King, the Queen; the ministers and privy councillors; the archbishop (who was the Grand Almoner), the bishops and the minor clergy; the maids-of-honour, ladies of the bedchamber, governesses, gentlemen-in-waiting, equerries, heralds, physicians, officers, masters of the household, cooks, scullions, lackeys, guards, Switzers, pages, footmen. She touched the Princess's tutors and the Court professors in the midst of their deep studies. She touched likewise all the horses in the stables, with the grooms; the huge mastiffs in the yard; even Tiny, the Princess's little pet dog, and Fluff, her black-and-white cat, that lay coiled on a cushion by her bedside.

She touched with her wand everything and everybody in the palace.

The instant the Fairy Hippolyta touched them they all fell
asleep, not to awake until the same moment as their mistress,
that all might be ready to wait on her when she needed them.
The very spits at the fire went to sleep, loaded as they were
with partridges and pheasants; and the fire went to sleep too.
All this was done in a moment: the Fairies were never long
about their business in those days.

But it so happened that one of the King's councillors, the
Minister of Marine (his office dated from a previous reign
when the kingdom had hoped to conquer and acquire a
seaboard) had overslept himself that morning and came late
to the palace without any knowledge of what had befallen. He
felt no great fear that his unpunctuality would be remarked,
the King (as he supposed) being absent in the country;
nevertheless he took the precaution of letting himself in by
a small postern door, and so missed being observed by the
Fairy and touched by her wand. Entering his office, and
perceiving that his under-secretary (usually so brisk) and
all his clerks rested their heads on their desks in attitudes of
sleep, he drew the conclusion that something had happened,
for he was an excellent judge of natural slumber. The farther
he penetrated into the palace, the stronger his suspicions
became. He withdrew on tiptoe. Though by nature and habit
a lazy man, he was capable of sudden decision, and returning
to his home he caused notices to be posted up, forbidding
any one to approach the castle, the inmates of which were
suffering from a rare but temporary affliction known as the
Sleeping Sickness.

These notices were unnecessary, for within a few hours
there grew up, all around the park, such a number of trees of
all sizes, and such a tangle of briars and undergrowth, that
neither beast nor man could find a passage. They grew until
nothing but the tops of the castle towers could be seen, and

these only from a good way off. There was no mistake about it: the Fairy had done her work well, and the Princess might sleep with no fear of visits from the inquisitive.

One day, many, many years afterwards, the incomparable young Prince Florimond happened to ride a-hunting on that side of the country which lay next to the tangled forest, and asked: 'What were those towers he saw pushing up above the midst of a great thick wood? '

They all answered him as they heard tell. Some said it was an old castle haunted by ghosts. Others, that all the wizards and witches of the country met there to keep Sabbath.

The most general opinion was that an Ogre dwelt there, and that he carried off thither all the children he could catch, to eat them at his ease. No one could follow him, for he alone knew how to find a passage through the briars and brambles. The Prince could not tell which to believe of all these informants, for all gave their versions with equal confidence, as commonly happens with those who talk on matters of which they can know nothing for certain. He was turning from one to another in perplexity, when a peasant spoke up and said: –

'Your Highness, long ago I heard my father tell that there was in yonder castle a Princess, the most beautiful that ever man saw; that she must lie asleep there for many, many years; and that one day she will be awakened by a King's son, for whom she was destined.'

At these words Prince Florimond felt himself a-fire. He believed, without weighing it, that he could accomplish this fine adventure; and, spurred on by love and ambition, he resolved to explore then and there and discover the truth for himself.

Leaping down from his horse he started to run towards the wood, and had almost reached the edge of it before the attendant courtiers guessed his design. They called to him to come back, but he ran on, and was about to fling himself boldly into the undergrowth, when as by magic all the great trees, the shrubs, the creepers, the ivies, briars and brambles, unlaced themselves of their own accord and drew aside to let him pass. He found himself within a long glade or avenue, at the end of which glimmered the walls of an old castle; and towards this he strode. It surprised him somewhat that none of his attendants were following him; the reason being that as soon as he had passed through it, the undergrowth drew close as ever again. He heard their voices, fainter and fainter behind him, beyond the barrier, calling, beseeching him to desist. But he held on his way without one backward look. He was a Prince, and young, and therefore valiant.

He came to the castle, and pushing aside the ivies that hung like a curtain over the gateway, entered a wide outer court and stood still for a moment, holding his breath, while his eyes travelled over a scene that might well have frozen them with terror. The court was silent, dreadfully silent; yet it was by no means empty. On all hands lay straight, stiff bodies of men and beasts, seemingly all dead. Nevertheless, as he continued to gaze, his courage returned; for the pimpled noses and ruddy faces of the Switzers told him that they were no worse than asleep; and their cups, which yet held a few heeltaps of wine, proved that they had fallen asleep over a drinking-bout.

He stepped by them and passed across a second great court paved with marble; he mounted a broad flight of marble steps leading to the main doorway; he entered a guardroom, just within the doorway, where the guards stood in rank with shouldered muskets, every man of them asleep and snoring his best. He made his way through a number of rooms filled with ladies and gentlemen, some standing, others sitting, but all asleep. He drew aside a heavy purple curtain, and once more held his breath; for he was looking into the great Hall of

State where, at a long table, sat and slumbered the King with his Council. The Lord Chancellor slept in the act of dipping pen into inkpot; the Archbishop in the act of taking snuff; and between the spectacles on the Archbishop's nose and the spectacles on the Lord Chancellor's a spider had spun a beautiful web.

Prince Florimond tiptoed very carefully past these august sleepers and, leaving the hall by another door, came to the foot of the grand staircase. Up this, too, he went; wandered along a corridor to his right, and, stopping by hazard at one of the many doors, opened it and looked into a bath-room lined with mirrors and having in its midst, sunk in the floor, a huge round basin of whitest porcelain wherein a spring of water bubbled deliciously. Three steps led down to the bath, and at the head of them stood a couch, with towels, and court-suit laid ready, exquisitely embroidered and complete to the daintiest of lace ruffles and the most delicate of body linen.

Then the Prince bethought him that he had ridden far before ever coming to the wood; and the mirrors told him that he was also somewhat travel-stained from his passage through it. So, having by this time learnt to accept any new wonder without question, he undressed himself and took a bath, which he thoroughly enjoyed. Nor was he altogether astonished, when he tried on the clothes, to find that they fitted him perfectly. Even the rosetted shoes of satin might have been made to his measure.

Having arrayed himself thus hardily, he resumed his quest along the corridor. The very next door he tried opened on a chamber all panelled with white and gold; and there, on a bed the curtains of which were drawn wide, he beheld the loveliest vision he had ever seen: a Princess, seemingly about seventeen or eighteen years old, and of a beauty so brilliant that he could not have believed this world held the like.

But she lay still, so still! ... Prince Florimond drew near, trembling and wondering, and sank on his knees beside her. Still she lay, scarcely seeming to breathe, and he bent and touched with his lips the little hand that rested, light as a rose-leaf, on the coverlet ...

With that, as the long spell of her enchantment came to an end, the Princess awaked; and looking at him with eyes more tender than a first sight of him might seem to excuse: –

'Is it you, my Prince?' she said. 'You have been a long while coming!'

The Prince, charmed by these words, and still more by the manner in which they were spoken, knew not how to find words for the bliss in his heart.

He bent and touched with his lips the little hand.

He assured her that he loved her better than his own self. Their speech after this was not very coherent; they gazed at one another for longer stretches than they talked; but if eloquence lacked, there was plenty of love. He, to be sure, showed the more embarrassment; and no need to wonder at this – she had had time to think over what to say to him; for I hold it not unlikely (though the story does not say anything of this) that the good Fairy Hippolyta had taken care to amuse her, during her long sleep, with some pleasurable dreams. In short, the Princess Aurora and the Prince Florimond conversed for four hours, and still without saying the half they had to say.

Meanwhile all the palace had awaked with the Princess. In the Council Chamber the King opened his eyes and requested the Lord Chancellor to read that last sentence of his over again a little more distinctly. The Lord Chancellor, dipping his quill into the dry inkpot, asked the Archbishop in a whisper how many t's there were in 'regrettable.' The Archbishop, taking a pinch of snuff that had long ago turned to dust, answered with a terrific sneeze, which again was drowned by the striking of all the clocks in the palace, as they started frantically to make up for lost time. Dogs barked, doors banged; the Princess's parrot screamed in his cage and was answered by the peacocks squawking from the terrace; amid which hubbub the Minister for Agriculture, forgetting his manners, made a trumpet of his hands and bawled across the table, begging His Majesty to adjourn for dinner. In short, every one's first thought was of his own business; and, as they were not all in love, they were ready to die with hunger.

Even the Queen, who had dropped asleep while discussing with her maids-of-honour the shade of mourning which most properly expressed regret for royal personages in a trance, lost her patience at length, and sent one of her attendants with word that she, for her part, was keen-set for something to eat, and that in her young days it had been customary for young ladies released from enchantment to accept the congratulations of their parents without loss of time. The Prince Florimond, by this message recalled to his devoirs, helped the Princess to rise. She was completely dressed, and very magnificently too.

Taking his beloved Princess Aurora by the hand, he led her to her parents, who embraced her passionately and – their first transports over – turned to welcome him as a son, being charmed (quite apart from their gratitude) by the modest gallantry of his address. They passed into a great dining-room lined with mirrors, where they supped and were served by the royal attendants. Violins and hautboys discoursed music that was ancient indeed, but excellent, and the meal was scarcely concluded before the company enjoyed a very pleasant surprise.

Prince Florimond, having no eyes but for his love, might be excused if he forgot that his attendants must, long before now, have carried home their report, and that his parents would be in deep distress, wondering what had become of him. But the King, the Princess's father, had a truly royal habit of remembering details, especially when it concerned setting folks at their ease. Before dinner he had dispatched a messenger to carry word to Prince Florimond's father, that his son was safe, and to acquaint him briefly with what had befallen. The messenger, riding through the undergrowth – which now obligingly parted before him as it had, a while ago, to admit the Prince – and arriving at the outskirts of the wood, found there a search-party vainly endeavouring to break through the barrier, with the Prince's aged father standing by and exhorting them in person, to whom he delivered his message. Trembling with relief – for he truly supposed his son to be lost beyond recall – the old man entreated the messenger to turn back and escort him. So he arrived, and was ushered into the hall.

The situation, to be sure, was delicate. But when these two kings, both so well meaning, had met and exchanged courtesies, and the one had raised the other by the hand to a place on the dais beside him, already and without speech they had almost accorded.

'I am an old man,' said the Prince's father; 'I have reigned long enough for my satisfaction, and now care for little in life but to see my son happy.'

'I think I can promise you that,' said the Princess's father, smiling, with a glance at the two lovers.

'I am old enough, at any rate, to have done with ambitions,' said the one.

'And I,' said the other, 'have dreamed long enough, at any rate, to despise them. What matters ruling to either of us two, while we see your son and my daughter reigning together?'

So it was agreed, then and there; and after supper, without loss of time, the Archbishop married the Prince Florimond and the Princess Aurora in the chapel of the Castle. The two Kings and the Princess's mother saw them to their chamber, and the first maid-of-honour drew the curtain. They slept little – the Princess had no occasion; but the Prince next morning led his bride back to the city, where they were acclaimed by the populace and lived happy ever after, reigning in prosperity and honour.

2

Cinderella

Once upon a time there lived a gentleman who married twice. His second wife was a widow with two grown-up daughters, both somewhat past their prime, and this woman would have been the proudest and most overbearing in the world had not her daughters exactly resembled her with their fine airs and insolent tempers. The husband, too, had by his first wife a child of his own, a young daughter, and so good and so gentle that she promised to grow up into the living image of her dead mother, who had been the most lovable of women.

The wedding festivities were no sooner over than the stepmother began to show herself in her true colours. She could not endure the girl's good qualities, which by contrast rendered her own daughters the more odious. She put her to drudge at the meanest household work, and thus she and her precious darlings not only wreaked their spite but saved money to buy themselves dresses and finery. It was the child who scoured the pots and pans, scrubbed the floors, washed down the stairs, polished the tables, ironed the linen, darned the stockings, and made the beds. She herself slept at the top of the house in a garret, upon a wretched straw mattress, while her sisters had apartments of their own with inlaid floors,

She put her to the meanest household work.

beds carved and gilded in the latest fashion, and mirrors in which they could see themselves from head to foot.

Yet they were so helpless, or rather they thought it so menial to do anything for themselves, that had they but a ribbon to tie, or a bow to adjust, or a bodice to be laced, the child must be sent for. When she came it was odds that they met her with a storm of abuse, in this fashion: –

'What do you mean, pray, by answering the bell in this state? Stand before the glass and look at yourself! Look at your hands – faugh! How can you suppose we should allow you to touch a ribbon, or even come near us, with such hands? Run downstairs and put yourself under the kitchen pump' – and so on.

'How can I help it?' thought the poor little drudge. 'If I do not run at once when the bell rings, they scold me for that. Yet they ring – both of them together sometimes – a minute after setting me to rake out a grate and sift the ashes. As for looking at myself in the glass, gladly would I do it if they allowed me one. But they have told me that if I had a glass I should only waste time in front of it.'

She kept these thoughts to herself, however, and suffered her ill-usage patiently, not daring to complain to her father, who would, moreover, have joined with the others in chiding her, for he was wholly under his wife's thumb; and she had enough of chiding already. When she had done her work she used to creep away to the chimney-corner and seat herself among the cinders, and from this the household name for her came to be Cinders; but the younger sister, who was not so ill-tempered as the elder, called her Cinderella. They were wise in their way to deprive her of a looking-glass; for in truth, and in spite of her sorry rags, Cinderella was a hundred times more beautiful than they with all their magnificent dresses.

It happened that the King's son gave a ball, and sent invitations through the kingdom to every person of quality. Our two misses were invited among the rest, for they cut a great figure in that part of the country. Mightily pleased they were to be sure with their cards of invitation, all printed in gold and stamped with the broad red seal of the Heir Apparent; and mightily busy they were, discussing what gowns and head-dresses would best become them. This meant more worry for Cinderella, for it was she who ironed them. They could talk of nothing but their ball dresses.

'For my part,' said the elder, 'I shall wear a red velvet dress – for she had a passion for crimson, and could not perceive how ill the colour went with her complexion. 'I had thought of cloth-of-gold, but there's the cost of the underskirt to be considered; and underskirts seem to grow dearer and dearer in these days. What a relief,' she went on, 'it must be to have money and not be forced to set one thing against another!'

'I,' said the younger, 'must make shift with my old underskirt; that is, unless I can wheedle some money out of

Papa' – for so, in their affection, they called their stepfather. 'Cinderella can take out the worst stains to-morrow. I believe that, if she tries, she can make it look as good as new; and, at all events, it will give her something to do instead of wasting an afternoon. I don't pretend that I like wearing an old underskirt, and I hope to make dear Papa sensible of this; but against it I shall have the gold-flowered robe, on which I am determined, and my diamond stomacher, which is somewhat better than the common.'

'And I, of course,' said the elder, 'must wear my diamond spray. If only it had a ruby in the clasp instead of a sapphire! Rubies go so much better with crimson ... I suppose there is no time now to ask the jeweller to re-set it with a ruby.'

'But you don't possess a ruby, dear,' murmured her sister, who did possess one, and had no intention of lending it. 'And, besides, sapphires suit you so much better!'

They sent for the best milliner they could find, to build their mob-caps in triple tiers; and for the best hairdresser to arrange their hair; and their patches were supplied by the shop to which all the Quality went. From time to time they called up Cinderella to ask her advice, for she had excellent taste. Cinderella advised them perfectly, and even offered her services to dress their hair for them on the night of the ball. They accepted gladly enough.

Whilst she was dressing them one asked her: 'Cinderella, would you not like to be going to the ball?'

'Alas! miss,' said Cinderella, 'you are making fun of me. It is not for the like of me to be there.'

'You are right, girl. Folks would laugh indeed to see Cinders at a ball!'

Any one but Cinderella would have pinned on their mob-caps awry; and if you or I had been in her place, I won't swear but that we might have pushed in the pins just a trifle carelessly. But she had no malice in her nature; she attired them to perfection, though they found fault with her all the while it was doing, and quite forgot to thank her when it was done. Let it be related, in excuse for their tempers, that they had passed almost two days without eating, so eager were they and excited. The most of this time they had spent in front of their mirrors, where they had broken more than a dozen laces in trying to squeeze their waists and make them appear more slender. They were dressed a full two hours before the time fixed for starting. But at length the coach arrived at the door. They were tucked into it with a hundred precautions, and Cinderella followed it with her eyes as long as she could; that is to say, until the tears rose and blinded them. She turned away weeping, back to the house, and crept into her dear chimney-corner; where, being all alone in the kitchen, she could indulge her misery.

A long while she sat there. Suddenly, between two heavy sobs she looked up, her eyes attracted by a strange blue glow on the far side of the hearth: and there stood the strangest lady, who must have entered somehow without knocking.

Her powdered hair was dressed all about her head in the prettiest of short curls, amid which the most exquisite jewels – diamonds, and rubies, and emeralds – sparkled against the firelight. Her dress had wide panniers bulging over a skirt of lace flounces, billowy and delicate as sea-foam, and a stiff bodice, shaped to the narrowest waist imaginable. Jewels flashed all over this dress – or at least Cinderella supposed them to be jewels, though, on second thoughts, they might be fireflies, butterflies, glowworms. They seemed at any rate to be alive, and to dart from one point to another of her attire. Lastly, this strange lady held in her right hand a short wand, on the end of which trembled a pale bluish-green flame; and it was this which had first caught Cinderella's eye and caused her to look up.

'Good evening, child,' said the visitor in a sharp clear voice, at the same time nodding kindly across the firelight. 'You seem to be in trouble. What is the matter?'

'I wish,' sobbed Cinderella. 'I wish,' she began again, and again she choked. This was all she could say for weeping.

'You wish, dear, that you could go to the ball; is it not so?'

'Ah, yes!' said Cinderella with a sigh.

'Well, then,' said the visitor, 'be a good girl, dry your tears, and I think it can be managed. I am your godmother, you must know, and in younger days your mother and I were very dear friends.' She omitted, perhaps purposely, to add that she was a Fairy; but Cinderella was soon to discover this too. 'Do you happen to have any pumpkins in the garden?' her godmother asked.

There stood the strangest lady.

Cinderella thought this an odd question. She could not imagine what pumpkins had to do with going to a ball. But she answered that there were plenty in the garden – a whole bed of them in fact. 'Then let us go out and have a look at them.'

They went out into the dark garden to the pumpkin patch, and her godmother pointed to the finest of all with her wand. 'Pick that one,' she commanded.

Cinderella picked it, still wondering. Her godmother opened a fruit knife that had a handle of mother-of-pearl. With this she scooped out the inside of the fruit till only the rind was left; then she tapped it with her wand, and at once the pumpkin was changed into a beautiful coach all covered with gold.

The pumpkin changed
into a beautiful coach.

'Next
we must have
horses,' said her
godmother. 'The question is, Have you such a thing as a mouse trap in the house?'

Cinderella ran to look into her mouse trap, where she found six mice all alive. Her godmother, following, told her to lift the door of the trap a little way, and as the mice ran out one by one she gave each a tap with her wand, and each mouse turned at once into a beautiful horse – which made a fine team of six horses, of a lovely grey, dappled with mouse colour.

Now the trouble was to find a coachman. 'I will go and see,' said Cinderella, who had dried her tears and was beginning to find this great fun, 'if there isn't such a thing as a rat in the rat trap. We can make a coachman of him.'

'You are right, dear,' said her godmother; 'run and look.'

Cinderella fetched her the rat trap. There were three large rats in it. The Fairy chose one of the three because of his enormous whiskers, and at a touch he was changed into a fat coachman.

Next she said: 'Go to the end of the garden; and there in the corner of the wall behind the watering-pot, unless I am mistaken, you will find six lizards. Bring them to me.'

Cinderella had no sooner brought them than her godmother changed them into six footmen, who climbed up at once behind the coach with their bedizened liveries, and clung on as though they had been doing nothing else all their lives.

The Fairy then said to Cinderella: 'Hey now, child! This will do to go to the ball with, unless you are hard to please.'

'Indeed, yes,' answered Cinderella. 'But how can I go, as I am, in these horrid clothes?'

'You might have given me credit for thinking of that too!' Her godmother did but touch her with her wand, and on the instant her rags were transformed into cloth of gold and silver, all bespangled with precious stones. She felt her hair creeping up into curls, and tiring and arranging itself in tiers, on the topmost of which a double ostrich feather grew from a diamond clasp that caught the rays of the old lady's wand and shot them about the garden, this way and that, making the slugs and snails crawl to shelter.

'But the chief mark of a lady,' said her godmother, eyeing her with approval, 'is to be well shod,' and so saying she pulled out a pair of glass slippers, into which Cinderella poked her toes doubtfully, for glass is not as a rule an accommodating material for slippers. You have to be measured very carefully for it.

Her rags were transformed.

But these fitted to perfection: and thus arrayed from top to toe, Cinderella had nothing more to do but kiss her godmother, thank her, and step into the coach, the six horses of which were pawing the cabbage beds impatiently.

'Good-bye, child! 'said her godmother. 'But of one thing I must warn you seriously. I have power to send you thus to the ball, but my power lasts only until midnight. Not an instant beyond midnight must you stay there. If you over-stay the stroke of twelve, your coach will become but a pumpkin again, your horses will change back into mice, your footmen into lizards, and your ball dress shrink to the same rags in which I found you.'

Cinderella promised that she would not fail to take her departure before midnight: and, with that, the coachman cracked his whip and she was driven away, beside herself with joy.

In the royal palace, and in the royal gardens, over which shone the same stars which had looked down upon Cinderella's pumpkins, the ball was at its height: with scores and scores of couples dancing on the waxed floor to the music of the violins; and under the trees, where the music throbbed in faint echoes, other scores of couples moving, passing and repassing, listening to the plash of the fountains and inhaling the sweet scent of the flowers.

Now, as the King's son walked among his guests, word was brought to him by his Chamberlain that a grand Princess, whom nobody knew, had just arrived and desired admission.

'She will not tell her name,' said the Chamberlain; 'but that she is a Princess and of very high dignity cannot be doubted. Apart from her beauty and the perfection of her address (of which your Royal Highness, perhaps, will allow me to be no mean judge), I may mention that the very jewels in her hair are worth a whole province.'

The King's son hastened to the gate to receive the fair stranger, handed her down from the coach, and led her through the gardens, where the guests drew apart and gazed in wonder at her loveliness. Still escorted by him she entered the ball-room, where at once a great silence fell, the dancing was broken off, the violins ceased to play – so taken, so ravished was everybody by the vision of this unknown one. Everywhere ran the murmur, 'Ah! how beautiful she is!' The King himself, old as he was, could not take his eyes off her, and confided to the Queen in a low voice that it was long since he had seen so adorable a creature.

All the ladies were busily studying her head-dress and her ball gown, that they might order the like next day for themselves, if only (vain hope!) they could find materials so exquisite and dressmakers clever enough.

The King's son took her to the place of honour, and afterwards led her out to dance. She danced so gracefully that all admired her yet the more. A splendid supper was served, but the young Prince ate nothing of it, so intent was he on gazing upon her.

She went and sat by her sisters, who bridled with pleasure at the honour. She did them a thousand civilities, sharing with them the nectarines and citrons which the Prince brought her; and still not recognising her, they

The King's son led her out to dance.

marvelled at this, being quite unused (as they never deserved) to be selected for attentions so flattering.

The King's son now claimed her for another dance. It had scarcely come to an end when Cinderella heard the clock strike the quarter to twelve; whereupon she instantly desired her partner to lead her to the King and Queen. 'For I must be going,' she said.

'It is cruel of you to go so early,' he protested. 'But at least you will come again to-morrow and grant me many dances?'

'Is there to be another ball, then, to-morrow?' she asked.

'To-morrow, yes; and as many morrows as you wish, if only you will come.'

'Ah, if I could!' sighed Cinderella to herself: for she was young, and it seemed to her that she could never have enough of such evenings as this, though they went on for ever and ever.

The Prince led her to the dais where sat the King and
Queen. She made a deep reverence before them, a slighter but
no less gracious one to the company, and withdrew. Although
she had given no orders, her coach stood waiting for her.
Slipping in, she was whisked home in the time it would take
you to wink an eye.

She had scarcely entered the house, however, before she
received a shock. For on the threshold of the kitchen, glancing
down to make sure that her ball gown was not disarranged
by this rapid journey, she perceived that it had vanished
– changed back to the rags of her daily wear. But there, in
the light of the hearth, stood her godmother, who smiled
so pleasantly that Cinderella choked down her little cry of
disappointment.

'Well, child? And how have you fared?'

'Godmama, I have never been so happy in all my life! And it
is all thanks to you!' But after thanking her, Cinderella could
not help confessing how she longed to go to the ball next
evening. The King's son had begged her to come again, and
oh! if she had been able to promise!

'As to that, child,' said her godmother, 'we will see about it
when the time comes. But it has been lonely, keeping watch
and sitting up for you. Will you not reward me by telling all
about it?'

Cinderella needed no such invitation; she was dying to
relate her adventures. She talked and talked, her godmother
still smiling and questioning. For two hours, may be, she
talked and was still recollecting a score of things to tell when
her sisters' coach rumbled up to the gate, and almost at once
there came a loud ring at the bell. She stared and rubbed her
eyes, for at the first sound of it her godmother had vanished!

Cinderella ran and opened the door to her sisters. 'What
a long time you have stayed,' said she, yawning, rubbing her

eyes, and stretching herself as though she had just waked out of sleep. (She had felt, however, no inclination at all to sleep since their departure!)

'If you had been at the ball,' said the elder sister, 'you would not have felt tired. One of the guests was the loveliest Princess – oh, the loveliest you ever could see! She showed us a thousand civilities. She gave us nectarines and citrons.'

Cinderella contained her joy. Upstairs, while she unplaited her sisters' hair and unlaced their bodices, she asked the name of the Princess. But they answered that no one knew her; that the King's son was wild about her, and would give everything in the world to discover who she was. Cinderella smiled. She no longer felt any temptation at all to be clumsy with the hairpins.

'Why then,' she said, 'she must be beautiful indeed. And she went away, you say, without telling her name? Is no one going to see her again?'

'As for that, she may come again to the ball to-morrow. I am told that the Prince begged it, almost with tears in his eyes. For there is to be another ball to-morrow, and we are going!'

'Ah, heavens!' sighed Cinderella, 'how lucky you are! Might I not just see her? Please, please, Sister Caroline, take me to-morrow – I could manage quite well if only you lent me your yellow gown which you wear every evening!'

'Hoity-toity!' snapped Miss Caroline. 'You cannot be awake. You must have been dreaming to some purpose if you see me lending my clothes to a nasty little Cinders!'

Cinderella had quite well expected some such rebuff, and was glad enough to get it, for it would have been very awkward if her sister had been willing to lend the gown.

The next evening the two sisters were at the ball; and so was Cinderella, but in even finer attire than before. Her godmother had spared no pains, and as for the expense, that hardly needs to be considered when you can turn pumpkins into gilt coaches, cobwebs into lace, and beetles' wings into rubies, with the tap of a wand.

The King's son in his impatience flew to her coach door as soon as she arrived. Throughout the evening he never left her side, nor ceased to make pretty speeches; and she, pretty maid, was far from finding his behaviour tiresome – so far, indeed, that she forgot her godmother's warning. The end was, that in the midst of a dance she heard the stroke of a clock, looked up, was dismayed to find it the first stroke of twelve when she believed it yet an hour short of midnight, and made her escape as lightly as a deer. The Prince followed, but could not catch her. Only she dropped one of her glass slippers, which he picked up and treasured.

With the last stroke of twelve, coach and footmen had whisked away, and poor Cinderella, barefoot now as well

She dropped one of her glass slippers.

as in rags, panted homeward over roads where the flints cut
her until she bled, and the owls and great moths blundered
out of the bushes against her face. To make matters worse,
a thunderstorm broke before she had ran half the distance,
and she arrived home in a terrible plight, muddy, drenched
to the skin, and almost more dead than alive. In one thing
only she was fortunate: she had outstripped her sisters, whose
coach on the way home lost a wheel – and I have a suspicion
that Cinderella's godmother had something to do with this
misadventure too. At all events, when Cinderella opened the
kitchen door the little lady stood as she had stood the night
before, in the glow of the hearth, awaiting her.

'Well, child,' she said, frowning, yet the frown was not
altogether unkindly, 'it is easily seen that you have forgotten
my warning and have suffered for it. But what is that you
are clutching?'

Poor Cinderella drew from under her bedraggled bodice
a crystal slipper, fellow to the missing one. It was the one
remnant of all her finery, and somehow, scarcely knowing
why, she had hugged it to her while she ran and never let it
slip in all her stumblings.

Her godmother gazed at her with a strange expression, that
began by being a frown, yet in the end had certainly changed
into a shrewd smile.

'You have been careless,' she said. 'Yet I am pleased to see
that you have managed to keep, at any rate, one-half of your
godmother's gift.' I think she meant by this that whereas all
the rest of Cinderella's adornment had been contrived out of
something other than it was, the two glass slippers had been
really produced out of the Fairy's pocket. They alone had not
vanished at the stroke of midnight. 'But what has become of
the other one?' her godmother asked.

Cinderella did not know for certain, but fancied that she must have dropped it in her hurry to escape from the palace.

'Yes, you are careless,' repeated the Fairy; 'but decidedly you are not unlucky.'

And with that she vanished, as the bell sounded announcing the sisters' return.

They were not in the best of humours, to begin with. Cinderella asked them if they had again found the ball enjoyable, and if the beautiful lady had been there. They told her yes; but that on the stroke of twelve she had taken flight, and so hurriedly that she had let fall one of her small glass slippers, the prettiest in the world, which the King's son had picked up. They added, that this indeed was the first cause of their delay; for, seeking their carriage, they had found the entry blocked, and the Prince in the wildest state of mind, demanding of the guards if they had not seen a Princess pass out. The guards answered that they had seen no one pass out but a ragged girl, who looked more like a country wench than a Princess. Amid this to-do, the sisters had with difficulty found their coach; and then, within two miles of home, a wheel had come off and the coach had lurched over, in a thunderstorm, too; and they had been forced to walk the rest of the way, the one with a bruised shoulder, and the other (which was worse) with a twisted ankle. But, after all, the dance had been worth these mischances and sufferings; and, said they, harking back, the Prince was undoubtedly deep in love, for they had left him gazing fondly at the slipper, and little doubt – mysteriously as she chose to behave – he would make every effort to find the beautiful creature to whom it belonged.

They told the truth, too. For a few days after, the King's son had it proclaimed by sound of trumpet that he would marry her whose foot the slipper exactly fitted.

At first they tried it on the Princesses of the Court:

Then on the Duchesses:

Then on the Marchionesses:

Then on the Countesses and Viscountesses:

Then on the Baronesses:

And so on, through all the ladies of the Court, and a number of competitors, who, though they did not belong to it, yet supposed that the smallness of their feet was an argument that their parents had very unjustly come down in the world. The Prime Minister, who carried the glass slipper on a velvet cushion, was kept very busy during the next few weeks.

At length he called on Cinderella's two sisters, who did all they could to squeeze a foot into the slipper, but by no means could they succeed.

Cinderella, who was looking on and admiring their efforts, said laughingly: –

'Let me see if it will fit me.'

Her sisters began to laugh and mock at her, but the Prime Minister, who had come to make trial of the slipper, looked at Cinderella attentively, and seeing how good-looking she was, said that it was but just – he had orders to try it upon every one. He asked Cinderella to sit down, and drawing the slipper upon her little foot, he saw that it went on easily, and fitted the foot like wax. Great was the astonishment of the two sisters; but it was greater when Cinderella pulled from her pocket the other little slipper and put it upon the other foot. On top of this came a rap at the door, and in walked the Fairy Godmother, who, by a touch of her wand upon Cinderella's clothes, made them still more magnificent than they had been before.

And now her two sisters knew Cinderella to be the same beautiful creature they had seen at the ball. They threw themselves at her feet, begging her pardon for all the ill-usage they had made her suffer. Cinderella raised and kissed them, saying that she forgave them with all her heart, and entreated them to be loving to her always.

They led her to the young Prince, arrayed as she was. He thought her lovelier than ever, and, a few days after, they were married. Cinderella, who was as good as she was beautiful, lodged her two sisters in the palace, and married them that same day to two great Lords of the Court.

The slipper went on easily.

3

Beauty and the Beast

Once upon a time, in a country a long way from here, there stood a flourishing city, full of commerce; and in that city lived a merchant so lucky in all his ventures that it seemed as if fortune waited on his wishes. But while enormously rich, he had a very long family of six sons and six daughters; and as yet not one of them was settled in life. The boys were too young to go out in the world; and the girls, who had everything at home the heart could desire, were in no hurry to risk a change by choosing a husband, although many rich and noble suitors paid court to them. But one day an unexpected disaster brought this pleasant state of things to an end. Their house caught fire and was burnt to the ground; and with it perished not only the magnificent furniture, but the merchant's account books, bank notes, gold and silver, and the precious wares on which his wealth depended. Scarcely anything was saved.

This was but the beginning of their misfortunes. Their father, who up to now had prospered in everything he touched, lost in a very short while every ship he had upon the sea. Some were wrecked, others captured by pirates. His agents failed; his clerks in foreign countries proved unfaithful;

Some were wrecked, others captured by pirates.

and, in short, from the height of riches he suddenly fell into the direst poverty.

Nothing was left to him but one poor little country cottage, at least a hundred leagues from the city in which he had lived. In this he was driven to find refuge, and to this he carried off his family, who were in despair since the overthrow. The daughters especially could not endure the thought of dwelling in such a den (as they called it). At first they had felt sure that on hearing the news their suitors would be tripping one another up in haste to renew their offers of marriage. But in this they were soon undeceived. Their downfall was no sooner known than all these flattering wooers took to their heels in a troop. They fared no better with their intimate friends, who at once dropped their acquaintance. Nay, those to whom our merchant had formerly shown the greatest kindness were now the most eager to speak ill of him.

So nothing was left for this hapless family but to take their departure from the city and shut themselves up in the cottage, which stood in the depth of a dismal and almost trackless forest. No servants now to wait on them! The sons tilled the ground and swept out the farm sheds; and the daughters, dressed like country girls in coarse linen frocks, were forced to turn their delicate hands to the roughest employment and live on hard fare of which there was little enough.

Only the youngest daughter showed a brave heart. She had been despondent as any of them to begin with; but after weeping – as well she might – for her father's misfortunes, she recovered her natural gaiety, made the best of things, tried to forget how ungrateful the world had been, kept her father and her brothers amused with her cheerful wit, and after she had done her work, would sing and play. But her sisters would not join with her in making the best of things. 'It is very easy for you to be happy,' the eldest grumbled. 'You have low tastes and were born for this kind of life.' The fact is, they were all jealous of her because of her sweet temper and good looks. So beautiful, indeed, was this youngest sister that in the old days every one had agreed to call her Beauty – by that and by no other name she was known. Alone of them she might easily, in the first days of their ruin, have found a husband; but she could not think of this while she could be of use to help and console her family.

Two years passed, and there came news which seemed to offer a hope to escape. One of their father's ships, long supposed to be lost, had arrived in port with a rich cargo. The message further advised his return to the city with speed, or his, agents might sell the goods too cheaply and he would lose his gains. So, whilst his children danced with joy at the news, the merchant set about preparing for his long journey.

In their transport his daughters loaded him with commissions for gowns and jewels it would have taken a fortune to buy. Only Beauty would not ask for anything. Her father, noting her silence, interrupted the others who still kept adding to their list of requirements.

'Well, Beauty,' he said, 'and what shall I bring home for you? Surely you, too, wish for something?'

'Dear father,' she answered, 'I wish for the most precious thing in the world; and that is to see you home again safe and sound.'

This answer covered the sisters with confusion, and vexed them so that one of them, speaking up for the others, said tartly: 'This small miss is putting on airs. She thinks, no doubt, she cuts a figure with her affected fine sentiments!'

Her father, however, was touched by her good feeling. Nevertheless he told her to choose something – 'For,' said he, 'at your age it is only natural to like dresses and pretty presents.'

'Well, dear father,' said she, 'since you insist, I will beg you to bring me home a rose. I have not seen one since we came to live here, and I love roses.' In this way Beauty contrived to obey her father and yet to put him to no expense.

The day came for the merchant to embrace them all and bid them farewell. He made the best of his way to the great city; and arrived there to be met with a great disappointment. To be sure his vessel had come safely to port; but his partners, believing him dead, had taken possession of it and divided the cargo between them. To make good his claim he was forced to bring a number of tedious law-suits. He won them in the end; but only to find, after six months of trouble and expense, that he was almost as poor as when he started.

To make his misery complete he was forced to travel back in the winter, in the most inclement weather; so that by the time he reached the skirts of the forest he was ready to drop with fatigue. But reminding himself that his home was now not many leagues away, he called up what strength remained to him. As he pushed on through the forest, night overtook him; and in the piercing cold, half buried – his horse and he – in the deep snow that hid every pathway, the poor merchant

feared that his last hour had come. Not so much as a hut did
he pass. The only shelter to be found was the trunk of a hollow
tree; and there he cowered through the long night, kept awake
by his hunger and the howling of the wolves. Nor did the day
bring him much comfort: for thick snow lay everywhere, and
not a path was to be seen. It was only after a weary search that
he managed to recover his horse, which had wandered
away and partly sheltered itself in another hollow tree.
He mounted, and now in a little while discovered
a sort of track which presently grew easier.

Following this, he found himself in an
avenue of trees, at the entrance of
which he halted and rubbed his
eyes. For no snow had fallen
in this avenue, and
the trees were tall
orange-trees,
planted in

As he pushed on through the
forest, night overtook him.

four rows and covered with flowers and fruit; and here and
there among the trees were statues, some of single figures,
others of groups representing scenes of war, but all coloured
like real life.

At the end of the avenue, straight in front of him, rose
a magnificent castle in many terraces. The merchant rode
around to the stable courtyard, which he found empty; and
there, with half-frozen hands, he unbridled and stabled his

horse. Within the doorway he found a staircase of agate with balusters of carved gold. He mounted it and passed through room after room, each more splendidly furnished than the last. They were deliciously warm, too, and he began to feel his limbs again. But he was hungry; where could he find some one to give him food? Everywhere was silence; and yet the place had no look of being abandoned. Drawing rooms, bedchambers, galleries – all stood unlocked. At last, tired of roaming, he came to a halt in an apartment where some one had lit a bright fire. A sofa drawn up cosily beside it, invited him to sit and warm his limbs; and resting there, he closed his eyes and fell into deep and grateful slumber.

As weariness had sent him to sleep, so hunger awoke him. He opened his eyes and saw at his elbow a table with meats and wine upon it. He had been fasting for more than twenty-four hours, and lost no time in falling-to. He hoped that he might soon have sight of this most hospitable entertainer, whoever he might be, and an opportunity of thanking him. Still no one appeared; and now this good food did for him what fatigue had done before. He dropped off again into an easy slumber which lasted for four hours almost. Again awaking, he saw at his elbow another small table – of porphyry this time – upon which the unknown hands had set out a dainty meal of cakes, crystallised fruits and liqueurs. To this, too, he did justice. But, as the time still passed and no one appeared, he began to feel terrified, and resolved to search once more through all the rooms. But still he found no one.

He was standing lost in thought, when of a sudden it came into his mind that some kindly power had perhaps prepared this palace of wonder for him, that it with all its riches might indeed be his. Possessed by this notion he once again made a tour of the rooms and took stock of their treasures, planning in his mind how he would divide them amongst his children, assigning this apartment to one and that to another, and whispering to himself what joy he would carry home after all from his journey. Then he went down into the garden, where – though it was the depth of winter – the birds were singing and the air breathed the scent of a thousand flowers.

'Surely,' he told himself, 'my daughters will be happy here and never desire any more to go back to the city. Quick! Let me saddle my horse at once and ride home with the news!'

The way to the stable was an alley fenced on either hand with palings, and over the palings hung great clusters of roses in bloom. They reminded him of his promise to Beauty. He plucked one, and was about to pluck a whole nosegay, when he was startled by a horrible noise behind him, and attempted to turn. But behind him stood a hideous Beast who was overtaking him and reaching out towards him.

'Who gave you leave to pluck my roses?' roared this monster. 'Was it not enough that I made you welcome in my palace and treated you kindly? And you show your gratitude by stealing my flowers! But your insolence shall not go unpunished!' The good merchant, terrified no less by the

Behind him stood a hideous Beast.

sight of this Beast than by his threats, let drop the rose and flung himself on his knees.

'My Lord,' he cried, 'have pity on me! I am not ungrateful; but after all your kindness I could not guess that so small a thing would offend you.'

This speech did not at all abate the Beast's wrath. 'Hold your tongue, sir,' he commanded, 'if you can offer me nothing but flatteries and false titles. I am not "my lord." I am the Beast; and your words will not save you from the death you deserve.'

The merchant, although in fear of his life, plucked up courage to tell the monster that the rose which he had been bold to pluck was for one of his daughters, by name Beauty. Then, in hope either to delay the Beast's vengeance or to touch his compassion, he launched into the tale of all his misfortunes, and of his reasons for the journey, not forgetting to mention Beauty again and her request.

The Beast considered for a moment before answering him in a somewhat milder tone: 'I will forgive you; but only on condition that you give me one of your daughters. Some one must make amends for this trespass.'

'Heaven forgive me,' the merchant entreated, 'but how can I promise such a thing! Even were I cruel enough to purchase my life at the cost of a child, on what excuse could I bring her?'

'No excuse is necessary,' replied the Beast shortly. 'Whichever you bring must come here of her own free will, or not at all. Go home and try if there be one brave and loving enough to sacrifice herself to save your life. You seem to be an honest man. Give me your word to return here at the end of a month and bring whichever of your daughters you can persuade to come with you. If you can persuade none of them, you must come alone; and I warn you that, if you fail of it, I shall come and fetch you.'

What was the poor man to do? He promised, for he saw death staring him in the face; and having given his promise he hoped to be allowed to depart. But the Beast informed him that he could not go until next day.

'Then,' said he, 'at daybreak you will find a horse ready for you who will carry you home in less than no time. Now go and eat your supper, and await my commands.'

The merchant, more dead than alive, crept back to his rooms. There, before a blazing fire, he found a delicious supper spread, inviting him to eat. But so distraught was he, that no food, however delicious, could have tempted him had he not been afraid that the Beast might be hiding somewhere to watch him. In fear of this he forced himself to sit and taste of the dishes.

A loud noise in the next room warned him that the Beast was coming. Since he could not escape, he mustered what courage he could to conceal his terror, and faced about to the doorway.

'Have you made a good supper?' was the Beast's first question.

The merchant in humblest voice answered that, thanks to his host's kind attention, he had fared excellently well.

'I am paying you a visit,' said the Beast, 'to warn you again to be honest with your daughter. Describe me to her just as I am. Let her be free to choose whether she will come or no; but tell her that, her course once chosen, there can be no retreat, nor even reflection after you have brought her to me. To break faith then will avail nothing: she will but destroy you without winning her own release.'

Again the spirit-broken merchant repeated his promise.

The Beast appeared to be content at length. 'Retire to bed now,' he commanded, 'and do not get up to-morrow until you see the sun and hear a golden bell rung. Then, before starting, you will find breakfast laid for you here; your horse will be standing ready saddled in the courtyard; and you may carry back the rose to your daughter Beauty – as you call her. For the rest, I count on seeing you back in a month's time. So, farewell.'

The merchant, who dared not disobey a single one of these orders, retired to bed at once, though without any temptation to sleep; and again, though he passed a wretched night, he was punctual to rise with the sun. A golden bell rang; and prompt on the sound he found breakfast laid, still by unseen hands. After breakfast he went down to the stables, and on his way paused to pick up the rose, which lay in the alley where it had dropped from his hand. It was fresh as ever, and smelt as sweetly as though it yet grew on the tree.

A few paces further on he found his horse standing ready saddled, with a handsome cloak of furs, far warmer than his own, lying across the saddle. He put it on and mounted, and now he had to wonder at yet another miracle. His horse set off at an incredible speed, so that before he could even turn in the saddle the palace had sunk out of sight.

Could the horse have felt the weight on the good man's mind, it had never made such a pace. But it took its own way, insensible to rein or bridle; nor halted until it reached the door of the cottage.

The merchant's sons and daughters had rushed out at his approach; though it was not until he drew quite close that they recognised their father in this horseman superbly cloaked, with a rose at his holster, and mounted on a horse that travelled at such a speed. When they recognised him, they made sure that he brought the best of news. But the tears that trickled down his cheeks as he dismounted told them another story.

His first motion then was to pluck the fatal rose from the pommel and hand it to Beauty, saying: 'Here is what you asked me to bring. You little know what it will cost you all.'

This, and his sorrowful look, gave the eldest daughter her cue. 'I was certain of it!' she said. 'Did I not say, all along, that to force a rose at this time of the year would cost you more than would have bought presents for all the rest of us? A rose, in mid-winter! And such a rose! There – one has only to look at it to see that you took good care Beauty should have her present, no matter at what cost to us!'

'It is all too true,' answered their father sorrowfully, 'that this rose has cost me dear – far dearer than all the presents you others begged of me. But the cost is not in money; for would to God I could have bought it with the last penny in my purse!'

His speech, you may be sure, excited their curiosity, and they gave him no rest until he had told the whole of his story. It left their hopes utterly dashed: and the daughters lamented their lot, while their brothers hardily declared that they would never allow their father to return to this accursed castle – they would march thither in a body and destroy the horrible Beast who owned it. But their father assured them that he had given his word and would rather die than break it.

Thereat the sisters turned upon Beauty and started to upbraid and rail against her.

'It is all your fault,' they declared; 'and this is what comes of your pretended modesty! Why could you not have asked for dresses and jewels as we did? Even if you could not get them, at least the demand would have cost nothing. But you chose to be singular – you, with your precious rose! And now our father must die, and we must all suffer through your affectation!'

Poor Beauty controlled her tears and answered them: 'Yes, I am to blame for all this, though, indeed, dear sisters, I did it innocently; for how could I guess that to ask for a rose in the middle of summer, as it was then, would give rise to all this misery? But what does that matter? Innocent or guilty,

I cannot allow you to suffer for what was my fault; and so I will go back with our father to save him from his promise. That will be in a month's time, and in this little month, I beg of you, let us be happy together without reproaches.'

At first her brothers would not hear of any such sacrifice, and her father was equally set against it, until the sisters again fired up in their jealousy and accused him of being distressed only because it happened to be Beauty; if another of his daughters (they hinted) had offered to pay this price for his life, he would have accepted it cheerfully enough!

Beauty closed this talk by saying firmly that, whether they wished it or not, she would go – 'And who knows,' said she, forcing a brave smile, 'but this fate of mine, which seems so terrible, may cover some extraordinary and happy fortune?' She said it merely to hearten them; but her sisters, fancying her deluded by vanity and self-conceit, smiled maliciously and applauded. So their father gave way, and it was agreed that Beauty must go. For her part she desired only that the few days remaining to her might be as happy as possible; and so, as they passed she spoke little of what was before her, and, if at all, only to treat it lightly and as a piece of good fortune. When the time drew near she shared up all her trinkets and little possessions with her sisters – for, badly as they had treated her, they were the only friends she had. Yet jealousy had made their hearts so wicked that when the fatal day arrived they actually rejoiced to hear the neighing of a horse which, punctually sent by the Beast, arrived at the door of the cottage.

The brothers would have rushed out and slain the beautiful animal; but Beauty, mastering their anger with a few tender words, bade her father mount into the saddle; and so, after bidding her sisters farewell with a tenderness that forced them to weep at the last, climbed to the pillion behind him quite as if she were setting out for a holiday. They were off! The horse seemed to fly rather than to gallop; so smoothly that Beauty could scarcely feel the motion save by the soft wind that beat on her cheek. Soon they caught sight of the castle in the distance. Her father, less happy than she, again and again asked and begged her to alight and return – a most idle offer, for he had no real control of the reins. But Beauty did not listen, because her mind was made up.

Nevertheless, she was awed, and all the more when, as the fleet horse galloped up to the courtyard, they were met by a great salvo of guns and, as the echoes died away, by the sound of soft music within the palace.

The horse had come to a stop, by a flight of agate steps; a light shone down these steps from a porchway within which the violins kept their throbbing. Beauty slipped down from the saddle, and her father, alighting after her, took her by the hand and led her to the chamber in which he had first supped; where, sure enough, they found a cheerful fire and a score of candles lit and burning with an exquisite perfume, and – best of all – a table laid with the daintiest of suppers.

The merchant, accustomed to the ways of their host, knew that the supper was meant for them, and Beauty fell-to with a good appetite. Her spirits indeed were rising. There had been no sign of any Beast in all the many rooms through which she had passed, and everything in them had seemed to breathe of gaiety and good living.

But this happy frame of mind did not last long. They had scarcely finished supper when the Beast was heard coming through the distant rooms. At the sound – the heavy padding of his feet, the roar of his breath – Beauty clung to her father in terror, and had almost fainted against the arm which he flung around her. But when the Beast stood before her in the doorway, after a little shudder she walked towards him

At the sound,
Beauty clung to her
father in terror.

with a firm step, and, halting at a little distance, saluted him respectfully. This behaviour evidently pleased the Beast. After letting his eyes rest on her face for a while, he said, in a tone that might well have struck terror into the boldest heart (and yet it did not seem to be angry): –

'Good evening, my good sir! Good evening, Beauty!'

The merchant was too far terrified to find his voice; but Beauty controlled hers and answered sweetly: –

'Good evening, Beast!'

'Have you come here of your own free will?' asked the Beast. 'And are you willing to let your father return and leave you here?'

Beauty answered that she was quite willing.

'Indeed? And yet what do you suppose will happen to you after he has gone?'

'Sir,' said Beauty, 'that is as it pleases you, and you only can tell.'

'Well answered,' replied the Beast; 'and since you have come of your own accord, you shall stay. As for you, my good sir,' said he to the merchant, 'you will take your departure at sunrise. The bell will give you warning; delay not to rise, eat your breakfast, and depart as before. But remember that you are forbidden ever to come within sight of my palace again.'

Then, turning to Beauty, he said: –

'Take your father into the next room, and choose between you everything you think will please your brothers and sisters. You will find there two travelling trunks: fill them as full as they will hold.'

Sorrowful as she was at the certainty of losing her father so soon and for ever, Beauty made ready to obey the Beast's orders, and he left them as he had come, saying: –

'Good night, Beauty! Good night, good sir!'

When they were alone, Beauty and her father went into the next room, which proved to be a store-chamber piled with treasures a king and queen might have envied. After choosing and setting apart in heaps, – one for each of her sisters, – the most magnificent dresses she could find, Beauty opened a cupboard which had a door of crystal framed in gold, and stood for a moment dazzled by the precious stones that lay piled on every shelf. After choosing a vast number and adding them to her heaps, she opened yet another wardrobe and found it full of money in gold pieces. This set her pondering.

'I think, father,' she said, 'that we had better empty these trunks again, and fill them with money. For money can always be turned to account, whereas to sell these precious stones you would have to go to some jeweller, who very likely would cheat you, and perhaps be suspicious of them. But with these pieces of gold you can buy land, houses, furniture, jewels – what you will – and no one will ask any questions.'

Her father agreed. Yet he
first of all tried to make
room for the money
by emptying out
the few things he
had packed for
himself. But this
was no good: for
it seemed that
the trunks were
made in folds
which opened
the wider the
more he put in.
Somehow the
more they packed,
the more room there
seemed to be, and they
ended by replacing all the
dresses and precious stones
they had taken out. But now the
trunks were so heavy that an elephant would
have sunk under them.

A chamber piled with treasures a king and queen might have envied.

'It is all a cheat!' cried the merchant. The Beast is mocking us, and only pretended to give us these things, knowing that I could not carry them away.'

'Wait a little,' advised Beauty. 'That would be a sorry jest, and I cannot help thinking that the Beast is honest; and that since he offered these gifts he will find you also the means to carry them. The best thing we can do is to strap up the trunks and leave them ready here.'

So they did this and went back to the little room, where to their amazement they found a breakfast laid on the table.

For a moment they could scarcely believe that the night had flown by whilst they were occupied in ransacking the treasure chamber and packing the trunks. But, glancing at the windows, they saw that day was indeed breaking; and presently a bell sounded, warning the merchant to eat quickly and depart.

He finished his meal, and they went down together to the courtyard, where two horses stood ready – the one laden with the two trunks, the other saddled for the merchant to ride. And now Beauty and her father would fain have spent a long time in bidding one another farewell. But the two horses neighed and pawed the ground so impatiently that he was afraid to linger. Tearing himself from his daughter's arms he mounted in haste, and could scarcely turn to say good-bye before both horses sprang away swift as the wind and he was lost to sight in an instant.

Poor Beauty! She gazed and gazed through her tears, and so mounted the stairs sorrowfully back to her own chamber. On reaching it she felt herself oppressed with sleepiness, for she had passed the night without undressing, and, moreover, for a month past her sleep had been broken and haunted with terrors. So, having nothing better to do, she went to bed, and was nestling down in the perfumed sheets when her eyes fell on the little table by the bedside. Some one had set a cup of hot chocolate there, and, half asleep, she reached out her hand for it and drank it; whereupon her eyes closed and she fell into a delicious slumber, such as she had not known since the day when her father brought home the fatal rose.

She dreamed that she was walking alongside an endless canal, the banks of which were bordered with tall orange-trees and myrtles in flower. There, as she wandered disconsolately lamenting her fate, of a sudden a young Prince stood before her. He was handsome as the God of Love in picture-books, and when he spoke it was with a voice that went straight to her heart. 'Dear Beauty,' he said, 'you are not so unfortunate as you suppose. It is here you shall find the reward of your goodness, denied to you elsewhere. Use your wits to find me out under the disguise which hides me – that is, if as I stand here now you find me not altogether contemptible. For I love you tenderly – you alone – and in making me happy you can attain to your own happiness. Beloved, never distrust your own true heart, and it shall lead you where the heart has nothing left to desire!' So saying, the charming apparition knelt at her feet, and again besought her to accept his devotion and become mistress over all his life.

'Ah! What can I do to make you happy?' she asked earnestly.

'Only be grateful,' he answered, 'and do not believe all that your eyes would tell you. Above all, do not abandon me until you have rescued me from the cruel sufferings I endure.'

With that the dream melted away, but only to be succeeded by another. She found herself face to face with a stately and beautiful lady; and the lady was speaking to her with dignity, yet most kindly.

'Dear Beauty,' she said, 'do not grieve for what you have left behind; a far higher destiny lies before you. Only, if you would deserve it, beware of being misled by appearances.'

Beauty found her dreams so agreeable that she was in no hurry at all to awake, and even when her eyes opened to the daylight she had more than half a mind to close them again. But a clock, chiming out her own name twelve times, warned her that it was midday and time to get up. She rose, therefore, and found her dressing-table set out with brushes and combs and everything she could want; and having dressed carefully, and with a lightness of heart for which she found it hard to account, she passed into the next room and found her dinner on the table.

Dinner does not take very long when you are all by yourself. Beauty, when she had eaten enough, sat down on a sofa and began to think of the handsome youth she had seen in her dream. 'He told me I could make him happy. Why, then, it must be that the horrible Beast, who appears to be master here, is keeping him a prisoner. How can I set him free? ... They both warned me not to trust to appearances. It is all very puzzling ... But one thing is clear at any rate, that I am very silly to be vexing my head over a dream. I will forget all about it, and look for something to do to amuse myself.'

She sprang up, and started to make a tour of discovery through the many rooms of the palace. They were even grander than she had expected. The first she entered was lined with mirrors from floor to ceiling, where she saw herself reflected on every side. The next thing to catch her eye was a bracelet, hanging from one of the chandeliers. Set in the bracelet was a gold locket, and opening this she was startled indeed; for it contained a portrait in miniature of the gallant youth she had seen in her dream. She could not be mistaken; so closely were his features engraved on her memory – yes, and, it may be, on her heart. She slipped the bracelet on her wrist, without stopping to think that it did not belong to her, and went on to explore further. She passed into a long picture gallery, and there again she met the Prince's face. It smiled down at her, this time from a life-sized portrait, and it seemed to smile so wistfully that she caught herself blushing.

From the gallery her steps had led her to a chamber filled with instruments of music. Beauty was an accomplished musician; so, sitting down, she amused herself by tuning and trying over one instrument after another; but she liked the harp best because that went best with her voice.

Leaving the music-room at length, she found herself in a long chamber like the picture gallery, but lined with books.

She started to make a tour of
discovery through the many
rooms of the palace.

It held an immense library; and Beauty, ever since she had
lived in the country, had been forced to do without reading,
for her father had sold all his books to pay his debts. Now, as
her eyes travelled along the shelves, she knew she need never
have any fear that time would pass heavily here. The dusk was
gathering before she had half-studied even the titles of the
thousands of volumes; and numbers of candles, waxen and
scented, in chandeliers with lustres of diamonds and rubies,
were beginning to light themselves in every room.

In due time Beauty found supper laid and served for her,
with the same good taste and orderliness as before, and
still she had seen no living face. What did this matter? Her
father had warned her that she would be solitary; and she
was beginning to tell herself that she could be solitary here
without much discomfort, when she heard the noise of the

Beast approaching. She could not help trembling a little; for she had not yet found herself alone with him, and knew not what would happen – he might even be coming to devour her. But when he appeared he did not seem at all ferocious.

'Good evening, Beauty,' he said gruffly.

'Good evening, Beast,' she answered gently, but shaking a little.

'Do you think you can be content here?' he asked.

Beauty answered politely that it ought not to be hard to live happily in such a beautiful palace.

After this they talked for an hour, and in the course of their talk Beauty began to excuse many things in the Beast – his voice, for example. With such a nose how could he help roaring through it? Really, he appeared to be wanting in tact rather than purposely terrible; though, to be sure, this want of tact terrified her cruelly, when at length he blurted out: –

'Will you be my wife, Beauty?'

'Ah! I am lost!' thought Beauty. The Beast could not be so dull-witted after all, for, though she kept the cry to herself, he answered quickly, and just as if she had uttered it aloud: –

'Not at all. I wish you to answer just "yes" or "no."'

'Oh! no, Beast.'

'Very well, then,' said this tractable monster. 'Since you will not, I had best be going. Good night, Beauty.'

'Good night, Beast,' answered Beauty, relieved of her fright. She felt sure now that he did not mean to hurt her, and as soon as he had taken his leave she went off to bed, and was asleep in no time. But almost as quickly she was dreaming, and in her dream at once she saw her unknown lover standing beside her, handsome as ever, but more sorrowful than before.

'Dear Beauty,' he said, 'why are you so cruel to me? I love you the better for being so stubborn, and yet it lengthens out my misery.'

She could not understand this at all. Her dream wavered and it seemed to her that he took a hundred different shapes in it. Now he had a crown between his hands and was offering it to her; now he was kneeling at her feet; now he smiled, radiant with joy; and again he buried his head in despair and wept till the sound of his sobbing pierced her heart. Thus, in one aspect or another, he was with her the night through. She awoke with him in her thoughts, and her first act was to unclasp the locket on her wrist and assure herself that the miniature was like him. It certainly was the same face, and his, too, was the face that smiled down from the larger portrait in the gallery. But the face in the locket gave her a more secret joy and she unclasped and gazed on it again and again.

This morning she went down into the gardens, where the sun shone inviting her to ramble. They were beyond imagination lovely. Here stood a statue showered over with roses; there fountain on fountain played and threw a refreshing spray so high in the air that her eyes could scarcely reach to its summit. But what most surprised her was that every nook and corner recalled those she had seen in her dreams with the unknown Prince standing beside her. At length she came to the long canal with the oranges and myrtles in the shade of which she had first seen him approach. It was the very spot, and she could no longer disbelieve that her dreams were real. She felt sure, now, that he must somehow be imprisoned here, and resolved to get at the truth that very evening, should the Beast repeat his visit.

Tired at length of wandering, she returned to the palace and discovered a new room full of materials for work to engage the most idle – tape-bags, distaffs and shuttles, frames for tapestry, ribbons to make into bows, silks for embroidery, scissors, and thimbles. Beyond this needlework room a door opened upon the most wonderful sight of all – an aviary full of the rarest birds, yet all so tame that they flew to Beauty, and perched themselves on her shoulders.

'Dear birds,' she said, 'I wish you were closer to my own room, that I might sit and hear you singing.'

She had scarcely said it when, opening a door beyond the aviary, she found herself in her own chamber – yes, her very own! – which she had thought to be quite on the other side of the building. The door, when she came to examine it, had a shutter which could be opened to hear, and closed again when she grew tired of it. This aviary opened on another inhabited by parrots, parroquets, and cockatoos. These no sooner saw Beauty than they began to scream and chatter; one wishing her 'Good morning,' another inviting her to luncheon, while a third yet more gallant cried 'Kiss me! Kiss me!' Others again whistled airs from grand opera or declaimed pieces of poetry by the best authors. It was plain that in their several ways they all had the same object – to amuse her.

Beyond the aviaries lay a monkey house. Here were apes of all sorts – Barbary apes, mandarin apes, apes with blue faces, baboons, marmosets, chimpanzees – and all came frisking about her, bowing and scraping, to show how much they appreciated the honour of this visit. To celebrate it they stretched a tight-rope and danced, and threw somersaults with an agility which Beauty found highly diverting; and yet she could not help sighing that none of these animals were able to tell her news of her unknown Prince Charming. She patted and made much of them, however, and asked if some of them would be kind enough to come with her and keep her company.

At once, and as if they had only been waiting for this command, two large she-apes in sweeping court-dresses stepped to her side and became her maids of honour; two brisk little marmosets volunteered for pages and held up her train; while an affable baboon, his face wreathed with smiles, bowed, presented a gloved hand, and begged leave to squire her. With this singular escort Beauty marched back to luncheon, and while she ate it the birds piped and fluted around her for accompaniment to the parrots, who lifted up their voices and chanted the latest and most fashionable tunes. Nay more; the meal was no sooner ended than the apes begged her to allow them to entertain her with a light comedy; which (leave being granted) they proceeded to act in a highly creditable manner and with appropriate dumb-show, while the parrots spoke the words from the wings very distinctly and in accents that exactly conformed with the various parts. At the close one of the actors advanced, laid his hand on his heart and – still with the parrot for interpreter – thanked Beauty for the indulgence she had shown to their poor efforts.

Two large she-apes in sweeping court-dresses stepped to her side.

That night again, after supper, the Beast paid her his accustomed visit. He put the same questions, and received her answers as before; and, as before, the conversation ended by his taking leave of her with a 'Good night, Beauty.' The two she-apes, as ladies-in-waiting, thereupon undressed their mistress and saw her to bed. Before leaving they thoughtfully opened the window-shutter, that the soft night-warbling of the birds might soothe her to sleep and dream of her lover.

In this fashion day followed day, and still Beauty found plenty to amuse her. At the end of a week she made the most wonderful discovery of all. There was one large room which she had entered but once, because it seemed to her rather dull, and dark too. It was empty; and although it had four windows in each wall, but two of them admitted any light. One day, as she passed the door, the fancy took her to open one of these windows. She stepped in and drew the shutter, when to her astonishment it opened, not upon daylight at all, but what seemed to be a dim hall lit only by a glimmer, distant and faint, behind the chinks of a thick curtain at the further end. She was wondering what this might mean, when the curtain went up and in a sudden flood of light she found herself gazing, as from a box, into a theatre crowded from floor to ceiling, and with an audience brilliant in dresses and jewels.

An orchestra played the overture, and gave place to the actors – real actors this time, not apes and parrots. The play was charming, and Beauty in ecstasy with every scene of it. When the curtain fell she still lingered in her box, hoping to see the fashionable crowd disperse; but somewhat to her chagrin the lights went out almost at once and the theatre was dark again. Still it had been very pleasant, and she promised herself to become a constant playgoer.

That evening when the Beast paid his visit, she told him all about the comedy. 'Eh? You like that sort of thing, do you?'

asked the monster. 'Well, you shall have as much of it as you like. You are so pretty.' Beauty could not help smiling inwardly at his clumsy compliments. But she smiled no longer when he put to her once again his blunt question: –

'Beauty, will you be my wife?'

'No, Beast,' she answered as before; but she was really beginning to get frightened, he was so gentle and so persistent. She sat up so long thinking over this that it was almost daylight before she closed her eyes in bed; and at once, as if impatient at being kept waiting, the lover of her dreams presented himself. Perhaps for this reason he was not in the best of tempers; at any rate he taxed her with being moody and discontented.

'I should be happy enough,' she answered, 'if the Beast did not pester me so. I – I almost think, by his foolish compliments, that he would like me to marry him.' Beauty expected her dream-lover to show some jealousy at this; seeing that he merely stood glum, she went on, 'Would you really be content if I married him?... but alas! no; were he as charming as he is hideous, you know that I love you and can never love any one else.' By all rights the Prince should have been in raptures at this avowal; but all his answer was: 'Dearest, love him who best loves you. Do not be led astray by appearances, and so you will free me from captivity.' This was not only puzzling; it seemed to Beauty to be just a little selfish. 'At least,' she said, 'tell me what to do! Since liberty appears to be your first wish, believe me, I would liberate you at any sacrifice, if only I knew how.' But this was what she could never discover; and because of it her nights now, though she longed for them, troubled her more than her days.

Her days passed pleasantly enough, and still in fresh discoveries. One by one in their turn she opened the windows of the great hall, and they revealed: –

First, a grand performance of Opera; and she listened not to the singers only, but to the murmur of the audience between the acts. To listen to this and to gaze on human faces, gave her an inexpressible pleasure.

Next, a great Fair in progress. When first she looked the throng had not arrived and she inspected the booths at leisure, with their various wares. As the spectators drifted in, the drums began to beat, the hobby horses to revolve, the showmen to shout, the marionettes to perform in their little theatre. It was ravishing.

After this she beheld a fashionable promenade, with a richly dressed crowd passing, re-passing, exchanging good-days, remarking how superb was the weather, and pausing to con and criticise the shop windows to right and left.

The next spectacle was a gaming-room, with the players seated at their cards or roulette, the croupiers spinning the ball or raking the money. Beauty, with nothing to stake, had leisure to observe their faces, and how sadly some left the tables who had come smiling with money in their pockets. She saw, too, that some were being cheated; and it vexed her, because she could not warn them.

Next, she was gazing at the Royal Palace, where the King and Queen were holding a reception. She saw ambassadors with their wives, lords and ladies and state counsellors; and watched them as they passed by the throne making their lowest bows.

A water picnic followed this. The boats lay moored alongside a bank where the merry-makers sat or lounged and talked to the sound of lutes.

The picnic ended in a ball, with violins playing and couples advancing and retreating on the waxed floor that shone in the light of a thousand candles. Oh, how Beauty longed to be one of the dancers!

But perhaps the last window gave her the most pleasure. For through it she was able to see the whole world at one gaze and all that was going on in it. State embassies, royal weddings, coronations, pageants, armies, revolutions, sieges, pitched battles – she could sit at her ease and watch them all, which was far more amusing than it is to read about them in a newspaper.

She ought, you will say, to have been happy as the day was long. But no: a life becomes flat and stale which is a perpetual round of pleasure and leaves nothing to sigh or to hope for. Beauty began to long for a sight of her father and her brothers and sisters. She concealed this for a while, however, and turned her thoughts to what was more pressing; for she could not beg leave to go home until something had been done to rescue her dear Unknown and restore him to liberty. The Beast alone (she reflected) could tell her the secret; and she thought to herself that, being himself so blunt of speech, he would forgive some bluntness in her. So one evening she asked him point-blank: 'Beast, are we alone in this palace, with nobody but ourselves?'

'Of course we are,' he answered gruffly; but the question appeared in some way to sting him, for almost at once he rose and bade her good night.

Now Beauty, whatever else she thought of the Beast, had by this time learnt to trust him for honest. It was a dreadful disappointment, therefore, to be forced to believe on his word that her Prince Charming had no existence outside of her fancy. She slept ill that night. In her dream she was wandering again and sorrowfully alongside the canal when her lover appeared and took her hands between his while he scanned her face all bathed in tears.

'What has gone wrong, dear Beauty?' he demanded. 'Why are you in this distress? ... Ah, it is the Beast who persecutes you! But, never fear, you shall be delivered here and now from his attention' – and with these words the Prince snatched out a dagger and rushed on the monster, who now for the first time came into the dream, advancing slowly down the bank of the canal. Strange to say, he offered no resistance even when the dagger almost touched his throat. But Beauty, whom an unseen power held back as she would have run to prevent the murder, on the instant found voice to cry, 'Stay! Stay, rash fool! or kill me before you kill him who has been my best friend!' 'Friend?' answered back the Prince, still with his dagger lifted; 'and am I no more than that?' 'You are an unfaithful one, at any rate,' persisted Beauty; 'if, knowing well that I would lay down my life for you, you would take the life of one who has done me so much kindness.' But while she pleaded the figures wavered in her dream, still struggling together, and vanished, giving place to the same stately lady she had seen in her former vision. 'Courage, Beauty!' said this fresh phantom; 'your happiness is not far off, if only you will go your own way and trust not to appearances.'

This dream left Beauty so uneasy that next day she opened one window after another to cure her restlessness; and, when this would not do, all the windows together; but still in vain. That night, when the Beast paid his usual visit, he detected almost at once that she had been weeping, and demanded the reason.

'Ah, sir,' said Beauty, 'if only I might go home!'

'You wish to go home?' The Beast's face turned pale – which, for such a face, was no easy matter. He staggered backwards with a deep sigh, or rather, a roar of grief. 'Ah, Beauty, Beauty! Would you desert a poor Beast? What more can I do to make you happy? Or is it because you hate me, that you wish to be gone?'

'No, Beast,' answered Beauty gently; 'I do not hate
you, and I should be very sorry never to see you
again. But I do long to see my own people. Let me
go home for two months only, and I promise to
come back and stay with you for the rest of
my life.'

The Beast had fallen flat and lay
along the carpet at her feet. His
eyes were closed, and for some
while his heavy sighs alone
told her that he was
neither dead nor in a
swoon. By and by he
lifted his head: –

He staggered backwards
with a roar of grief.

'I can deny you nothing,'
he said sadly. 'But no matter, though it cost me my
life ... In the room next to your bedroom you will find four
chests: fill them with everything you would like to take with
you. Be sure to keep your word; for if you break it and come
back to find your poor Beast dead, you will be sorry when it
is too late. Come back at the end of two months and you will
find me alive; and to come back you will not need chariot
or horses. Only say good-bye, that night, to your father, and
brothers, and sisters; and, when you are in-bed, turn this ring
round on your finger and say firmly: "I wish to go back to

my palace and see my Beast again." That is all. Good night, Beauty! Sleep soundly, and in good time you shall see your father once more.'

As soon as he was gone Beauty set to work to fill the four boxes with all the riches and finery that heart could desire. She filled them to the brim; and then, tired out, she went to bed. But for a long while she could not close her eyes for excitement. It was not until close upon sunrise that sleep visited her and, with it, another dream. In this dream she saw her beloved Unknown stretched at full length on a bank of turf. His face was hidden, and she could hear that he was sobbing. But when, touched by the sight of his grief, she drew near to console him, he lifted his face to her and said: –

'Cruel Beauty, how can you ask what ails me? when you are leaving me, and your going is my death warrant!'

'But, dearest Prince,' said Beauty, 'I am only going to tell my father and brothers and sisters that I am well and happy. In a short while I shall be back, never to leave you again ... But, for that matter,' she went on as a new thought struck her, 'why should we be separated at all? I will put off my going for another day, and to-morrow I will beg the Beast to let you go with me. I am sure he will not refuse.'

'I can only go with you, if you promise me never to come back,' replied the Prince. 'And, after all, when you have once delivered me, why should we ever come back? The Beast will be hurt in his feelings and very angry no doubt; but by that time we shall be beyond his power.'

'You forget,' Beauty reminded him sharply, 'that I have promised him to return, and that, moreover, he says he will die of grief if I break my word.'

'And what if he does?' demanded her lover. 'Is not your happiness worth more than the life of a monster? Of what use is he in the world except to frighten folks out of their wits?'

'Ah, you do not understand!' cried Beauty. 'This monster – as you call him – is only a monster in his face, and through no fault of his. He has the kindest heart in the world, and how could I be so ungrateful after all he has done for me!'

'I believe,' said her lover bitterly, 'that if you saw us fighting, of the two you would rather let me perish than this Beast of yours.'

Beauty told him that he was cruel and unjust, and begged him to talk of something else. She set the example, too. Seeing that he was piqued and proud, she addressed a long speech to him, full of endearments, to win him back to a good humour, and was growing astonished at her own eloquence when, in the middle of it, she awoke.

Her last words seemed to mingle with the sound of familiar voices. She sprang out of bed and drew her curtain ... It was very strange! As the sunlight poured in she saw that she was in a room much more poorly furnished than that in which she had fallen asleep. She dressed in haste, and opening the door, found that the next room too was like no apartment in the Beast's palace. But at her feet stood the four chests she had packed overnight; and, while she marvelled, again she heard a voice talking, and ran towards it. For it was her father's.

She rushed out and fell into his arms. He, poor man, stared at her as though she had sprung from another world, and the others were no less astonished. Her brothers embraced her with transports of joy, while her sisters – who, to tell the truth, had not overcome their jealousy – pretended to be quite as glad. They plied her with a thousand questions, which she answered very good-naturedly, putting aside her own impatience; for she too had a number of questions to ask. To begin with, this house of theirs was not the cottage in which she had left them, but a fine new one her father had been able to buy with the Beast's presents. If not wealthy, he was in easy circumstances; with the bettering of their fortunes his sisters had found other wooers and were soon to be married; and altogether Beauty had the satisfaction of knowing that she had at least brought prosperity back to her family. 'As for you, my dearest child,' said the merchant, 'when your sisters are married, you shall keep house for your brothers and me, and so my old age will be happy.'

This was all very well, but Beauty had to tell her father that she must leave him again in two months' time; whereat he broke out into lamentations. 'Dear father,' said the sensible girl, 'it is good of you to weep; but it is useless, and I would rather have your advice, which is sure to be useful.' Thereupon she told him all the story. Her father considered for a while, and then said: –

'I can only give you the same counsel that, by your own admission, you are always receiving from these phantoms of your dreams. "Do not trust to appearance," they say, and "Be guided by your heart's gratitude"; and they tell you this over and over again. What can it mean, child, but one thing? The Beast, you say, is frightful. His appearance is certainly against him. Then judge him rather by the gratitude which you certainly owe him. It is plain that he has a good heart – "handsome is as handsome does" – it is clear to me that these phantoms would have you say "Yes" to the Beast, and I too advise you to consent.'

Beauty saw the wisdom of this and knew very well that her father was counselling her for the best. Nevertheless it needed something more than this to reconcile her with marrying a monster, and she felt relieved at the thought that for two whole months she could put off deciding. Strange to say, as the days went by and the time of her departure drew nearer, she found herself looking forward to it rather than repining.

For one thing distressed her and spoilt all her happiness – she never dreamed at all now.

The days went by, and as they drew to an end her brothers and even her father (forgetting his former good counsel) employed all persuasions to hinder her departure. But her mind was made up; and when the two months were passed she was resolute on everything but the hour of her parting. Every morning, when she got up, she meant to say good-bye, but somehow another night came and the farewells were still unspoken.

She reproached herself (as well she might), and was still thus cruelly torn between two minds, when one night a dream visited her – the first for two months and more.

She dreamed that she was back at the Beast's palace, and wandering by a lonely path in the gardens which ended in a tangle of brushwood overhanging a cave. As she drew nearer she heard a terrible groaning, and running in haste she found the Beast stretched there on the point of death. Still in her dream she was bending over him when the stately lady stepped forth from the bushes and addressed her in a tone of grave reproach: –

'I doubt, Beauty, if even now you have come in time. Cruel, cruel of you to delay! when your delay has brought him so near to death!'

Terrified by this dream Beauty awoke in her bed with a start. 'I have done wickedly!' she cried. 'Am I too late? Oh, indeed I hope not!' She turned the ring upon her finger and said aloud in a firm voice: 'I wish to go back to my palace and see my Beast again!'

With that she at once fell asleep, and only woke up to hear the clock chiming, 'Beauty, Beauty,' twelve times on the musical note she so well remembered. She was back, then, at the palace. Yes, and – oh, joy! – her faithful apes and parrots were gathered around the bed, wishing her good morning!

She found the Beast stretched there on the point of death.

But none of them could tell her any news of the Beast. They were here to serve her, and all their thoughts ended with their duty. Their good master – the lord of this splendid palace – what was he to them? At any rate nothing was to be learnt from them, and Beauty was no sooner dressed than she broke away impatiently, wandering through the house and the gardens to fill up the time until evening should bring his accustomed visit. But it was hard work filling up the time. She went into the great hall and resolutely opened the windows one by one. The shows were there as before; but opera and comedy, fête and pageant, held no meaning for her: the players were listless, the music was null, the processions passed before her eyes but had lost their power to amuse.

Supper-time came at length; but when after supper the minutes passed and passed and still no Beast appeared, then indeed Beauty was frightened. For a long while she waited, listened, told herself this and that, and finally in a terror rushed down into the gardens to seek for him. The alleys were dark; the bushes daunted her with their black shadows; but still up and down ran poor Beauty, calling to the Beast, and calling in vain.

She was drenched with the dew, utterly lost and weary, when, after three hours, pausing for a moment's rest, she saw before her the same solitary path she had seen in her dream: and there in the moonlight she almost stumbled over the Beast.

He lay there, stretched at full length and asleep – or so she thought. So glad was she to have found him that she knelt and stroked his head, calling him by name over and over. But his flesh was cold beneath her hand, nor did he move or open his eyes.

'Ah, he is dead!' she cried, aghast.

But she put a hand over his heart, and to her inexpressible joy she felt that it was still beating. Hastily she ran to a fountain near by, and dipping water into her palms from its basin she ran and sprinkled it on his face, coaxing him with tender words as his eyes opened, and slowly – very slowly – he came to himself.

'Ah! what a fright you have given me!' she murmured. 'Dear Beast, I never knew how I loved you until I feared that you were dead – yes, dead, and through my fault! But I believe, if you had died, I should have died too.'

'Beauty,' said the Beast faintly, 'you are very good if indeed you can love such an ugly brute as I am. It is true that I was dying for you, and should have died if you had not come. I thought you had forsaken me. But are you sure?'

'Sure of what?' asked Beauty.

'That you love me?'

'Let us go back to supper,' said Beauty, raising his head.

'Yes, let us go back to supper,' agreed the Beast, lifting himself heavily on her arm. He still leaned on her, as they walked back to the palace together. But the supper – which they found laid for two – seemed to revive him, and in his old stupid way he asked her about the time she had spent at home, and if her father and brothers and sisters had been glad to see her.

Beauty, though weary enough after her search through the park and gardens, brisked herself up to tell of all that had happened to her in her absence. The Beast sat nodding his head and listening in his old dull way – which somehow seemed to her the most comfortable way in the world. At length he rose to go. But at the doorway he put the old blunt question.

'Beauty, will you marry me?'

'Yes, dear Beast,' said Beauty; and as she said it a blaze of light filled the room. A salvo of artillery sounded, a moment later, from the park. Bang, bang! fireworks shot across the windows of the palace; sky rockets and Roman candles exploded and a magnificent set-piece wrote across the darkness in letters of fire – 'long live beauty and the beast!'

Beauty turned to ask what all these rejoicings might mean; and, with that, she gave a cry. The Beast had vanished, and in his place stood the beloved Prince of her dreams! He smiled and stretched out his hands to her. Scarcely knowing what she did, she was stretching hers, to take them, when above the banging of fireworks in the avenues there sounded a rolling of wheels. It drew to the porch, and presently there entered the stately lady she had seen in her dreams. It was the very same; and, all astounded as she was, Beauty did reverence to her.

But the stately lady was as eager to do reverence to Beauty. 'Best and dearest,' said she, 'my son is going to love you always; as how should he not, seeing that by your courage you have rescued him from the enchantment under which he has lain so long, and have restored him to his natural form? But suffer also his mother, a Queen, to bless you!'

Beauty turned again to her lover and saw that he, who had been a Beast, was indeed the Prince of her dreams and handsomer than the day. So they were married and lived happy ever after; nay, so happy were they that all over the world folks told one another and set down in writing this wonderful history of Beauty and the Beast.

In his place stood the beloved Prince of her dreams.

4

Aladdin

There once lived a poor tailor, who had a son called Aladdin, a careless, idle boy who would do nothing but play all day long in the streets with little idle boys like himself. This so grieved the father that he died; yet, in spite of his mother's tears and prayers, Aladdin did not mend his ways. One day, when he was playing in the streets as usual, a stranger asked him his age, and if he was not the son of Mustapha the tailor. 'I am, sir,' replied Aladdin; 'but he died a long while ago.'

On this the stranger, who was a famous magician, fell on his neck and kissed him saying: 'I am your uncle, and knew you from your likeness to my brother. Go to your mother and tell her I am coming.'

Aladdin ran home and told his mother of his newly found uncle.

'Indeed, child,' she said, 'your father had a brother, but I always thought he was dead.' However, she prepared supper, and bade Aladdin seek his uncle, who came laden with wine and fruit. He fell down and kissed the place where Mustapha used to sit, bidding Aladdin's mother not to be surprised at not having seen him before, as he had been forty years out of the country. He then turned to Aladdin, and asked him his trade, at which the boy hung his head, while his mother burst into tears. On learning that Aladdin was idle and would learn no trade, he offered to take a shop for him and stock it with merchandise. Next day he bought Aladdin a fine suit of clothes and took him all over the city, showing him the sights, and brought him home at nightfall to his mother, who was overjoyed to see her son so fine.

Next day the magician led Aladdin into some beautiful gardens a long way outside the city gates. They sat down by a fountain and the magician pulled a cake from his belt, which he divided between them. Then they journeyed onwards till they almost reached the mountains. Aladdin was so tired that he begged to go back, but the magician beguiled him with pleasant stories and lead him on in spite of himself. At last they came to two mountains divided by a narrow valley. 'We will go no farther,' said his uncle. 'I will show you something wonderful; only do you gather up sticks while I kindle a fire.' When it was lit the magician threw on it a powder he had about him, at the same time saying some magical words. The earth trembled a little in front of them, disclosing a square flat stone with a brass ring in the middle to raise it by.

Aladdin tried to run away, but the magician caught him and gave him a blow that knocked him down. 'What have I done, uncle?' he said piteously; whereupon the magician said more kindly: 'Fear nothing, but obey me. Beneath this stone lies a treasure which is to be yours, and no one else may touch it, so you must do exactly as I tell you.'

At the word treasure Aladdin forgot his fears, and grasped the ring as he was told, saying the names of his father and grandfather. The stone came up quite easily, and some steps appeared. 'Go down,' said the magician; 'at the foot of those steps you will find an open door leading into three large halls. Tuck up your gown and go through them without touching anything, or you will die instantly. These halls lead into a garden of fine fruit trees. Walk on till you come to niche in a terrace where stands a lighted lamp. Pour out the oil it contains, and bring it me.' He drew a ring from his finger and gave it to Aladdin, bidding him prosper.

"Go down," said the magician.

Aladdin found everything as the magician had said, gathered some fruit off the trees, and, having got the lamp, arrived at the mouth of the cave. The magician cried out in a great hurry: 'Make haste and give me the lamp.' This Aladdin refused to do until he was out of the cave. The magician flew into a terrible passion, and throwing some more powder on to the fire, he said something, and the stone rolled back into its place.

The man left the country, which plainly showed that he was no uncle of Aladdin's but a cunning magician, who had read in his magic books of a wonderful lamp, which would make him the most powerful man in the world. Though he alone knew where to find it, he could only receive it from the hand of another. He had picked out the foolish Aladdin for this purpose, intending to get the lamp and kill him afterwards.

For two days Aladdin remained in the dark, crying and lamenting. At last he clasped his hands in prayer, and in so doing rubbed the ring, which the magician had forgotten to take from him. Immediately an enormous and frightful genie rose out of the earth, saying: 'What wouldst thou with me? I am the Slave of the Ring, and will obey thee in all things.'

Aladdin fearlessly replied, 'Deliver me from this place!' whereupon the earth opened, and he found himself outside. As soon as his eyes could bear the light he went home, but fainted on the threshold. When he came to himself he told his mother what had passed, and showed her the lamp and the fruits he had gathered in the garden, which were in reality precious stones. He then asked for some food.

'Alas! child,' she said, 'I have nothing in the house, but I have spun a little cotton and will go sell it.'

Aladdin bade her keep her cotton, for he would sell the lamp instead. As it was very dirty, she began to rub it, that it might fetch a higher price. Instantly a hideous genie appeared, and asked what she would have. She fainted away, but Aladdin, snatching the lamp, said boldly: 'Fetch me something to eat!' The genie returned with a silver bowl, twelve silver plates containing rich meats, two silver cups, and two bottles of wine.

Aladdin's mother, when she came to herself, said: 'Whence comes this splendid feast?'

'Ask not, but eat,' replied Aladdin. So they sat at breakfast till it was dinner-time, and Aladdin told his mother about the lamp. She begged him to sell it, and have nothing to do with devils. 'No,' said Aladdin, 'since chance hath made us aware of its virtues, we will use it, and the ring likewise, which I shall always wear on my finger.' When they had eaten all the genie had brought, Aladdin sold one of the silver plates, and so on until none were left. He then had recourse to the genie, who gave him another set of plates, and thus they lived many years.

Immediately an enormous and frightful genie rose out of the earth.

One day Aladdin heard an order from the Sultan proclaimed that everyone was to stay at home and close his shutters while the Princess his daughter went to and from the bath. Aladdin was seized by a desire to see her face, which was very difficult, as she always went veiled. He hid himself behind the door of the bath, and peeped through a chink. The Princess lifted her veil as she went in, and looked so beautiful that Aladdin fell in love with her at first sight. He went home so changed that his mother was frightened. He told her he loved the Princess so deeply he could not live without her, and meant to ask her in marriage of her father. His mother, on hearing this, burst out laughing, but Aladdin at last prevailed upon her to go before the Sultan and carry his request. She fetched a napkin and laid in it the magic fruits from the enchanted garden, which sparkled and shone like the most beautiful jewels. She took these with her to please the Sultan, and set out, trusting in the lamp. The Grand Vizier and the lords of council had just gone in as she entered the hall and placed herself in front of the Sultan. He, however, took no notice of her. She went every day for a week, and stood in the same place.

When the council broke up on the sixth day the Sultan said to his Vizier: 'I see a certain woman in the audience-chamber every day carrying something in a napkin. Call her next time, that I may find out what she wants.' Next day, at a sign from the Vizier, she went up to the foot of the throne and remained kneeling until the Sultan said to her: 'Rise, good woman, and tell me what you want.'

She hesitated, so the Sultan sent away all but the Vizier, and bade her speak freely, promising to forgive her beforehand for anything she might say. She then told him of her son's violent love for the Princess. 'I prayed him to forget her,' she said, 'but in vain; he threatened to do some desperate deed if I refused to go and ask your Majesty for the hand of the Princess. Now I pray you to forgive not me alone, but my son Aladdin.'

The Sultan asked her kindly what she had in the napkin, whereupon she unfolded the jewels and presented them. He was thunderstruck, and turning to the Vizier, said: 'What sayest thou? Ought I not to bestow the Princess on one who values her at such a price?'

The Vizier, who wanted her for his own son, begged the Sultan to withhold her for three months, in the course of which he hoped his son could contrive to make him a richer present. The Sultan granted this, and told Aladdin's mother

She went up to the foot of the throne.

that, though he consented to the marriage, she must not appear before him again for three months.

Aladdin waited patiently for nearly three months, but after two had elapsed, his mother, going into the city to buy oil, found everyone rejoicing, and asked what was going on. 'Do you not know,' was the answer, 'that the son of the Grand Vizier is to marry the Sultan's daughter tonight?'

Breathless she ran and told Aladdin, who was overwhelmed at first, but presently bethought him of the lamp. He rubbed it and the genie appeared, saying: 'What is thy will?'

Aladdin replied: 'The Sultan, as thou knowest, has broken his promise to me, and the Vizier's son is to have the Princess. My command is that to-night you bring hither the bride and bridegroom.'

'Master, I obey,' said the genie.

Aladdin then went to his chamber, where, sure enough, at midnight the genie transported the bed containing the Vizier's son and the Princess. 'Take this new-married man,' he said, 'and put him outside in the cold, and return at daybreak.'

Whereupon the genie took the Vizier's son out of bed, leaving Aladdin with the Princess.

'Fear nothing,' Aladdin said to her; 'you are my wife, promised to me by your unjust father, and no harm will come to you.' The Princess was too frightened to speak, and passed the most miserable night of her life, while Aladdin lay down beside her and slept soundly. At the appointed hour the genie fetched in the shivering bridegroom, laid him in his place, and transported the bed back to the palace.

Presently the Sultan came to wish his daughter good-morning. The unhappy Vizier's son jumped up and hid himself, while the Princess would not say a word and was very sorrowful. The Sultan sent her mother to her, who said: 'How comes

The genie took the Vizier's son out of bed.

it, child, that you will not speak to your father? What has happened?' The Princess sighed deeply, and at last told her mother how, during the night, the bed had been carried into some strange house, and what had passed there. Her mother did not believe her in the least, but bade her rise and consider it an idle dream.

The following night exactly the same thing happened, and next morning, on the Princess's refusing to speak, the Sultan threatened to cut off her head. She then confessed all, bidding him ask the Vizier's son if it were not so. The Sultan told the Vizier to ask his son, who owned the truth, adding that, dearly as he loved the Princess, he had rather die than go through another such fearful night, and wished to be separated from her. His wish was granted, and there was an end of feasting and rejoicing.

When the three months were over, Aladdin sent his mother to remind the Sultan of his promise. She stood in the same place as before, and the Sultan, who had forgotten Aladdin, at once remembered him, and sent for her. On seeing her poverty the Sultan felt less inclined than ever to keep his word, and asked his Vizier's advice, who counselled him to set so high a value on the Princess that no man living would come up to it. The Sultan than turned to Aladdin's mother, saying: 'Good woman, a sultan must remember his promises, and I will remember mine, but your son must first send me forty basins of gold brimful of jewels, carried by forty slaves, led by forty more, splendidly dressed. Tell him that I await his answer.'

The mother of Aladdin bowed low and went home, thinking all was lost. She gave Aladdin the message adding, 'He may wait long enough for your answer!'

'Not so long, mother, as you think,' her son replied. 'I would do a great deal more than that for the Princess.' He summoned the genie, and in a few moments the eighty slaves arrived, and filled up the small house and garden. Aladdin made them set out to the palace, two by two, followed by his mother. They were so richly dressed, with such splendid jewels, that everyone crowded to see them and the basins of gold they carried on their heads. They entered the palace, and, after kneeling before the Sultan, stood in a half-circle round the throne with their arms crossed, while Aladdin's mother presented them to the Sultan.

He hesitated no longer, but said: 'Good woman, return and tell your son that I wait for him with open arms.' She lost no time in telling Aladdin, bidding him make haste.

But Aladdin first called the genie. 'I want a scented bath,' he said, 'a richly embroidered habit, a horse surpassing the Sultan's, and twenty slaves to attend me. Besides this, six slaves, beautifully dressed, to wait on my mother; and lastly, ten thousand pieces of gold in ten purses.' No sooner said then done. Aladdin mounted his horse and passed through the streets, the slaves strewing gold as they went. Those who had played with him in his childhood knew him not, he had grown so handsome.

When the sultan saw him he came down from his throne, embraced him, and led him into a hall where a feast was spread, intending to marry him to the Princess that very day.

But Aladdin refused, saying, 'I must build a palace fit for her,' and took his leave. Once home, he said to the genie: 'Build me a palace of the finest marble, set with jasper, agate, and other precious stones. In the middle you shall build me a large hall with a dome, its four walls of massy gold and silver, each side having six windows, whose lattices, all except one which is to be left unfinished, must be set with diamonds and rubies. There must be stables and horses and grooms and slaves; go and see about it!'

The palace was finished the next day, and the genie carried him there and showed him all his orders faithfully carried out, even to the laying of a velvet carpet from Aladdin's palace to the Sultan's. Aladdin's mother then dressed herself carefully, and walked to the palace with her slaves, while he followed her on horseback. The Sultan sent musicians with trumpets and cymbals to meet them, so that the air resounded with

Aladdin ran to receive her.

music and cheers. She was taken to the Princess, who saluted her and treated her with great honour. At night the Princess said good-bye to her father, and set out on the carpet for Aladdin's palace, with his mother at her side, and followed by the hundred slaves. She was charmed at the sight of Aladdin, who ran to receive her. 'Princess,' he said, 'blame your beauty for my boldness if I have displeased you.' She told him that, having seen him, she willingly obeyed her father in this matter. After the wedding had taken place, Aladdin led her into the hall, where a feast was spread, and she supped with him, after which they danced till midnight.

Next day Aladdin invited the Sultan to see the palace. On entering the hall with the four-and-twenty windows with their rubies, diamonds and emeralds, he cried, 'It is a world's wonder! There is only one thing that surprises me. Was it by accident that one window was left unfinished?'

'No, sir, by design,' returned Aladdin. 'I wished your Majesty to have the glory of finishing this palace.'

The Sultan was pleased, and sent for the best jewellers in the city. He showed them the unfinished window, and bade them fit it up like the others. 'Sir,' replied their spokesman, 'we cannot find jewels enough.' The Sultan had his own fetched, which they soon used, but to no purpose, for in a month's time the work was not half done. Aladdin knowing that their task was vain, bade them undo their work and carry the jewels back, and the genie finished the window at his command. The Sultan was surprised to receive his jewels again, and visited Aladdin, who showed him the window finished. The Sultan embraced him, the envious Vizier meanwhile hinting that it was the work of enchantment.

Aladdin had won the hearts of the people by his gentle bearing. He was made captain of the Sultan's armies, and won several battles for him, but remained as courteous as before, and lived thus in peace and content for several years.

But far away in Africa the magician remembered Aladdin, and by his magic arts discovered that Aladdin, instead of perishing miserably in the cave, had escaped, and had married a Princess, with whom he was living in great honour and wealth. He knew that the poor tailor's son could only have accomplished this by means of the lamp, and travelled night and day till he reached the capital of China, bent on Aladdin's ruin. As he passed through the town he heard people talking everywhere about a marvellous palace. 'Forgive my ignorance,' he asked, 'what is the palace you speak of?'

'Have you not heard of Prince Aladdin's palace,' was the reply, 'the greatest wonder in the world? I will direct you if you have a mind to see it.' The magician thanked him who spoke, and having seen the palace knew that it had been raised by the Genie of the Lamp, and became half mad with rage. He determined to get hold of the lamp, and again plunge Aladdin into the deepest poverty.

Unluckily, Aladdin had gone a-hunting for eight days, which gave the magician plenty of time. He bought a dozen lamps, put them into a basket, and went to the palace, crying: 'New lamps for old!' followed by a jeering crowd. The Princess, sitting in the hall of four-and-twenty windows, sent a slave to find out what the noise was about, who came back laughing, so that the Princess scolded her.

'Madam,' replied the slave, 'who can help laughing to see an old fool offering to exchange fine new lamps for old ones?'

Another slave, hearing this, said, 'There is an old one on the cornice there which he can have.'

Now this was the magic lamp, which Aladdin had left there, as he could not take it out hunting with him. The Princess, not knowing its value, laughingly bade the slave take it and make the exchange. She went and said to the magician: 'Give me a new lamp for this.' He snatched it and bade the slave take her choice, amid the jeers of the crowd. Little he cared, but left off crying his lamps, and went out of the city gates to a lonely place, where he remained till nightfall, when he pulled out the lamp and rubbed it. The genie appeared, and at the magician's command carried him, together with the palace and the Princess in it, to a lonely place in Africa.

Next morning the Sultan looked out of the window towards Aladdin's palace and rubbed his eyes, for it was gone. He sent for the Vizier and asked what had become of the palace. The Vizier looked out too, and was lost in astonishment. He again put it down to enchantment, and this time the Sultan believed him, and sent thirty men on horseback to fetch Aladdin back in chains. They met him riding home, bound him, and forced him to go with them on foot. The people, however, who loved him, followed, armed, to see that he came to no harm. He was carried before the Sultan, who ordered the executioner to cut off his head. The executioner made Aladdin kneel down, bandaged his eyes, and raised his scimitar to strike.

At that instant the Vizier, who saw that the crowd had forced their way into the courtyard and were scaling the walls to rescue Aladdin, called to the executioner to stay his hand. The people, indeed, looked so threatening that the Sultan gave way and ordered Aladdin to be unbound, and pardoned him in the sight of the crowd.

Aladdin now begged to know what he had done.

'False wretch!' said the Sultan, 'come hither,' and showed him from the window the place where his palace had stood. Aladdin was so amazed he could not say a word. 'Where is your palace and my daughter?' demanded the Sultan. 'For the first I am not so deeply concerned, but my daughter I must have, and you must find her or lose your head.' Aladdin begged for forty days in which to find her, promising if he failed to

The executioner made Aladdin kneel down.

return to suffer death at the Sultan's pleasure. His prayer was granted, and he went forth sadly from the Sultan's presence.

For three days he wandered about like a madman, asking everyone what had become of his palace, but they only laughed and pitied him. He came to the banks of a river, and knelt down to say his prayers before throwing himself in. In doing so he rubbed the ring he still wore. The genie he had seen in the cave appeared, and asked his will.

'Save my life, genie,' said Aladdin, 'and bring my palace back.'

'That is not in my power,' said the genie; 'I am only the Slave of the Ring; you must ask him of the lamp.'

'Even so,' said Aladdin, 'but thou canst take me to the palace, and set me down under my dear wife's window.' He at once found himself in Africa, under the window of the Princess, and fell asleep out of sheer weariness.

He was awakened by the singing of the birds, and his heart was lighter. He saw plainly that all his misfortunes were owning to the loss of the lamp, and vainly wondered who had robbed him of it.

That morning the Princess rose earlier than she had done since she had been carried into Africa by the magician, whose company she was forced to endure once a day. She, however, treated him so harshly that he dared not live there altogether. As she was dressing, one of her women looked out and saw Aladdin. The Princess ran and opened the window, and at the noise she made, Aladdin looked up. She called to him to come to her, and great was the joy of these lovers at seeing each other again.

After he had kissed her Aladdin said: 'I beg of you, Princess, in God's name, before we speak of anything else, for your own sake and mine, tell me what has become of an old lamp I left on the cornice in the hall of four-and-twenty windows when I went a-hunting.'

'Alas,' she said, 'I am the innocent cause of our sorrows,' and told him of the exchange of the lamp.

'Now I know,' cried Aladdin, 'that we have to thank the magician for this! Where is the lamp?'

'He carries it about with him,' said the Princess. 'I know, for he pulled it out of his breast to show me. He wishes me to break my faith with you and marry him, saying that you were beheaded by my father's command. He is forever speaking ill of you, but I only reply by my tears. If I persist, I doubt not but he will use violence.'

Aladdin comforted her, and left her for a while. He changed clothes with the first person he met in the town, and having bought a certain powder returned to the Princess, who let him in by a little side door. 'Put on your most beautiful dress,' he said to her, 'and receive the magician with smiles, leading him to believe that you have forgotten me. Invite him to sup with you, and say you wish to taste the wine of his country. He will go for some, and while he is gone I will tell you what to do.'

She listened carefully to Aladdin and when he left her, arrayed herself gaily for the first time since she left China. She put on a belt and head-dress of diamonds and seeing in a glass that she was more beautiful than ever, received the magician, saying, to his great amazement: 'I have made up my mind that Aladdin is dead, and that all my tears will not bring him back to me, so I am resolved to mourn no more, and have therefore invited you to sup with me; but I am tired of the wines of China, and would fain taste those of Africa.'

The magician flew to his cellar, and the Princess put the powder Aladdin had given her in her cup. When he returned she asked him to drink her health in the wine of Africa, handing him her cup in exchange for his, as a sign she was reconciled to him. Before drinking the magician made her a speech in praise of her beauty, but the Princess cut him short, saying: 'Let us drink first, and you shall say what you will afterwards.' She set her cup to her lips and kept it there, while the magician drained his to the dregs and fell back lifeless. The Princess then opened the door to Aladdin, and flung her arms around his neck; but Aladdin went to the dead magician, took the lamp out of his vest, and bade the genie carry the palace and all in it back to China. This was done, and the Princess in her chamber felt only two little shocks, and little thought she was home again.

The Sultan, who was sitting in his closet, mourning for his lost daughter, happened to look up, and rubbed his eyes, for there stood the palace as before! He hastened thither, and Aladdin received him in the hall of the four-and-twenty windows, with the Princess at his side. Aladdin told him what had happened, and

The magician drained his cup and fell back lifeless.

showed him the dead body of the magician, that he might believe. A ten days' feast was proclaimed, and it seemed as if Aladdin might now live the rest of his life in peace; but it was not meant to be.

The magician had a younger brother, who was, if possible, more wicked and more cunning than himself. He travelled to China to avenge his brother's death, and went to visit a pious woman called Fatima, thinking she might be of use to him. He entered her cell and clapped a dagger to her breast, telling her to rise and do his bidding on pain of death. He changed clothes with her, put on her veil, and murdered her, that she might tell no tales. Then he went towards the palace of Aladdin, and all the people, thinking he was the holy woman, gathered round him, kissing his hands and begging his blessing. When he got to the palace there was such a noise going on round him that the Princess bade her slave look out the window and ask what was the matter. The slave said it was the holy woman, curing people by her touch of their ailments, whereupon the Princess, who had long desired to see Fatima, sent for her.

On coming to the Princess the magician offered up a prayer for her health and prosperity. When he had done the Princess made him sit by her, and begged him to stay with her always. The false Fatima, who wished for nothing better, consented, but kept his veil down for fear of discovery. The Princess showed him the hall, and asked him what he thought of it.

'It is truly beautiful,' said the false Fatima. 'In my mind it wants but one thing.'

'And what is that?' said the Princess.

'If only a roc's egg,' replied he, 'were hung up from the middle of this dome, it would be the wonder of the world.'

After this the Princess could think of nothing but the roc's egg, and when Aladdin returned from hunting he found her

The magician had a younger brother, more wicked and more cunning.

in a very ill humour. He begged to know what was amiss, and she told him that all her pleasure in the hall was spoilt for want of a roc's egg hanging from the dome.

'If that is all,' replied Aladdin, 'you shall soon be happy.' He left her and rubbed the lamp, and when the genie appeared commanded him to bring a roc's egg. The genie gave such a loud and terrible shriek that the hall shook.

'Wretch!' he cried, 'is it not enough that I have done everything for you, but you must command me to bring my master and hang him up in the midst of this dome? You and your wife and your palace deserve to be burnt to ashes, but that this request does not come from you, but from the brother of the magician, whom you destroyed. He is now in your palace disguised as the holy woman, whom he murdered. He it was who put that wish into your wife's head. Take care of yourself, for he means to kill you.' So saying, the genie disappeared.

Aladdin went back to the Princess, saying his head ached, and requesting that the holy Fatima should be fetched to lay her hands on it. But when the magician came near, Aladdin, seizing his dagger, pierced him to the heart.

'What have you done?' cried the Princess. 'You have killed the holy woman!'

'Not so,' replied Aladdin, 'but a wicked magician,' and told her of how she had been deceived.

After this Aladdin and his wife lived in peace. He succeeded the Sultan when he died, and reigned for many years, leaving behind him a long line of kings.

Aladdin, seizing his dagger, pierced him to the heart.

5

Snow White

It was the middle of winter, when the broad flakes of snow were falling around, that the queen of a country many thousand miles off sat working at her window. The frame of the window was made of fine black ebony, and as she sat looking out upon the snow, she pricked her finger, and three drops of blood fell upon it. Then she gazed thoughtfully upon the red drops that sprinkled the white snow, and said, 'Would that my little daughter may be as white as that snow, as red as that blood, and as black as this ebony windowframe!' And so the little girl really did grow up; her skin was as white as snow, her cheeks as rosy as the blood, and her hair as black as ebony; and she was called Snowdrop.

But this queen died; and the king soon married another wife, who became queen, and was very beautiful, but so vain that she could not bear to think that anyone could be handsomer than she was. She had a fairy looking-glass, to which she used to go, and then she would gaze upon herself in it, and say:

'Tell me, glass, tell me true!
Of all the ladies in the land,
Who is fairest, tell me, who?'

And the glass had always answered:

'Thou, queen, art the fairest in all the land.'

But Snowdrop grew more and more
beautiful; and when she was seven
years old she was as bright as
the day, and fairer than the
queen herself. Then the
glass one day answered the
queen, when she went to
look in it as usual:

'Thou, queen, art fair,
and beauteous to see,
But Snowdrop is
lovelier far than thee!'

When she heard this she
turned pale with rage and
envy, and called to one
of her servants, and said,
'Take Snowdrop away into
the wide wood, that I may
never see her any more.' Then the
servant led her away; but his heart
melted when Snowdrop begged him to
spare her life, and he said, 'I will not hurt you, thou pretty
child.' So he left her by herself; and though he thought it most
likely that the wild beasts would tear her in pieces, he felt as if
a great weight were taken off his heart when he had made up
his mind not to kill her but to leave her to her fate, with the
chance of someone finding and saving her.

The Queen had a
fairy looking-glass.

Then poor Snowdrop wandered along through the wood in great fear; and the wild beasts roared about her, but none did her any harm. In the evening she came to a cottage among the hills, and went in to rest, for her little feet would carry her no further. Everything was spruce and neat in the cottage: on the table was spread a white cloth, and there were seven little plates, seven little loaves, and seven little glasses with wine in them; and seven knives and forks laid in order; and by the wall stood seven little beds. As she was very hungry, she picked a little piece of each loaf and drank a very little wine out of each glass; and after that she thought she would lie down and rest. So she tried all the little beds; but one was too long, and another was too short, till at last the seventh suited her: and there she laid herself down and went to sleep.

By and by in came the masters of the cottage. Now they were seven little dwarfs, that lived among the mountains, and dug and searched for gold. They lighted up their seven lamps, and saw at once that all was not right. The first said, 'Who has been sitting on my stool?' The second, 'Who has been eating off my plate?' The third, 'Who has been picking my bread?' The fourth, 'Who has been meddling with my spoon?' The fifth, 'Who has been handling my fork?' The sixth, 'Who has been cutting with my knife?' The seventh, 'Who has been drinking my wine?' Then the first looked round and said, 'Who has been lying on my bed?' And the rest came running to him, and everyone cried out that somebody had been upon his bed. But the seventh saw Snowdrop, and called all his brethren to come and see her; and they cried out with wonder and astonishment and brought their lamps to look at her, and said, 'Good heavens! what a lovely child she is!' And they were very glad to see her, and took care not to wake her; and the seventh dwarf slept an hour with each of the other dwarfs in turn, till the night was gone.

Seven little dwarfs.

In the morning Snowdrop told them all her story; and they pitied her, and said if she would keep all things in order, and cook and wash and knit and spin for them, she might stay where she was, and they would take good care of her. Then they went out all day long to their work, seeking for gold and silver in the mountains: but Snowdrop was left at home; and they warned her, and said, 'The queen will soon find out where you are, so take care and let no one in.'

But the queen, now that she thought Snowdrop was dead, believed that she must be the handsomest lady in the land; and she went to her glass and said:

'Tell me, glass, tell me true!
Of all the ladies in the land,
Who is fairest, tell me, who?'

And the glass answered:

'Thou, queen, art the fairest in all this land:
But over the hills, in the greenwood shade,
Where the seven dwarfs their dwelling have made,
There Snowdrop is hiding her head; and she
Is lovelier far, O queen! than thee.'

Then the queen was very much frightened; for she knew that
the glass always spoke the truth, and was sure that the servant
had betrayed her. And she could not bear to think that anyone
lived who was more beautiful than she was; so she dressed
herself up as an old pedlar, and went her way over the hills,
to the place where the dwarfs dwelt. Then she knocked at the
door, and cried, 'Fine wares to sell!'

Snowdrop looked out at the window, and said, 'Good day,
good woman! what have you to sell?'

'Good wares, fine wares,' said she; 'laces and bobbins of
all colours.'

'I will let the old lady in; she seems to be a very good sort
of body,' thought Snowdrop, as she ran down and unbolted
the door.

'Bless me!' said the old woman, 'how badly your stays are
laced! Let me lace them up with one of my nice new laces.'
Snowdrop did not dream of any mischief; so she stood before
the old woman; but she set to work so nimbly, and pulled the
lace so tight, that Snowdrop's breath was stopped, and she fell
down as if she were dead. 'There's an end to all thy beauty,' said
the spiteful queen, and went away home.

In the evening the seven dwarfs came home; and I need
not say how grieved they were to see their faithful Snowdrop
stretched out upon the ground, as if she was quite dead.
However, they lifted her up, and when they found what
ailed her, they cut the lace; and in a little time she began to

breathe, and very soon came to life again. Then they said, 'The old woman was the queen herself; take care another time, and let no one in when we are away.'

When the queen got home, she went straight to her glass, and spoke to it as before; but to her great grief it still said:

'Thou, queen, art the fairest in
all this land:
But over the hills, in the greenwood shade,
Where the seven dwarfs their dwelling have made,
There Snowdrop is hiding her head; and she
Is lovelier far, O queen! than thee.'

Then the blood ran cold in her heart with spite and malice, to see that Snowdrop still lived; and she dressed herself up again, but in quite another dress from the one she wore before, and took with her a poisoned comb. When she reached the dwarfs' cottage, she knocked at the door, and cried, 'Fine wares to sell!'

But Snowdrop said, 'I dare not let anyone in.'

Then the queen said, 'Only look at my beautiful combs!' and gave her the poisoned one. And it looked so pretty, that she took it up and put it into her hair to try it; but the moment it touched her head, the poison was so powerful that she fell down senseless. 'There you may lie,' said the queen, and went her way. But by good luck the dwarfs came in very early that evening; and when they saw Snowdrop lying on the ground, they thought what had happened, and soon found the poisoned comb. And when they took it away she got well, and told them all that had passed; and they warned her once more not to open the door to anyone.

She took with her a poisoned comb.

Meantime the queen went home to her glass, and shook with rage when she read the very same answer as before; and she said, 'Snowdrop shall die, if it cost me my life.' So she went by herself into her chamber, and got ready a poisoned apple: the outside looked very rosy and tempting, but whoever tasted it was sure to die. Then she dressed herself up as a peasant's wife, and travelled over the hills to the dwarfs' cottage, and knocked at the door; but Snowdrop put her head out of the window and said, 'I dare not let anyone in, for the dwarfs have told me not.'

'Do as you please,' said the old woman, 'but at any rate take this pretty apple; I will give it you.'

'No,' said Snowdrop, 'I dare not take it.'

'You silly girl!' answered the other, 'what are you afraid of? Do you think it is poisoned? Come! do you eat one part, and I will eat the other.' Now the apple was so made up that one side was good, though the other side was poisoned. Then Snowdrop was much tempted to taste, for the apple looked so very nice; and when she saw the old woman eat, she could wait no longer. But she had scarcely put the piece into her mouth, when she fell down dead upon the ground. 'This time nothing will save thee,' said the queen; and she went home to her glass, and at last it said:

Take this pretty apple.

'Thou, queen,
art the fairest of
all the fair.'

And then her
wicked heart was
glad, and as happy as
such a heart could be.

When evening came,
and the dwarfs had gone home,
they found Snowdrop lying on the
ground: no breath came from her lips, and they were afraid that she was quite dead. They lifted her up, and combed her hair, and washed her face with wine and water; but all was in vain, for the little girl seemed quite dead. So they laid her down upon a bier, and all seven watched and bewailed her three whole days; and then they thought they would bury

her: but her cheeks were still rosy; and her face looked just as it did while she was alive; so they said, 'We will never bury her in the cold ground.' And they made a coffin of glass, so that they might still look at her, and wrote upon it in golden letters what her name was, and that she was a king's daughter. And the coffin was set among the hills, and one of the dwarfs always sat by it and watched. And the birds of the air came too, and bemoaned Snowdrop; and first of all came an owl, and then a raven, and at last a dove, and sat by her side.

And thus Snowdrop lay for a long, long time, and still only looked as though she was asleep; for she was even now as white as snow, and as red as blood, and as black as ebony. At last a prince came and called at the dwarfs' house; and he saw Snowdrop, and read what was written in golden letters. Then he offered the dwarfs money, and prayed and besought them to let him take her away; but they said, 'We will not part with her for all the gold in the world.' At last, however, they had pity on him, and gave him the coffin; but the moment he lifted it up to carry it home with him, the piece of apple fell from between her lips, and Snowdrop awoke, and said, 'Where am I?' And the prince said, 'Thou art quite safe with me.'

At last a prince came.

Then he told her all that had happened, and said, 'I love you far better than all the world; so come with me to my father's palace, and you shall be my wife.' And Snowdrop consented, and went home with the prince; and everything was got ready with great pomp and splendour for their wedding.

To the feast was asked, among the rest, Snowdrop's old enemy the queen; and as she was dressing herself in fine rich clothes, she looked in the glass and said:

'Tell me, glass, tell me true!
Of all the ladies in the land,
Who is fairest, tell me, who?'

And the glass answered:

'Thou, lady, art loveliest here, I ween;
But lovelier far is the new-made queen.'

When she heard this she started with rage; but her envy and curiosity were so great, that she could not help setting out to see the bride. And when she got there, and saw that it was no other than Snowdrop, who, as she thought, had been dead a long while, she choked with rage, and fell down and died: but Snowdrop and the prince lived and reigned happily over that land many, many years; and sometimes they went up into the mountains, and paid a visit to the little dwarfs, who had been so kind to Snowdrop in her time of need.

6

Hansel and Gretel

Hard by a great forest dwelt a poor wood-cutter with his wife and his two children. The boy was called Hansel and the girl Gretel. He had little to bite and to break, and once when great dearth fell on the land, he could no longer procure even daily bread. Now when he thought over this by night in his bed, and tossed about in his anxiety, he groaned and said to his wife: 'What is to become of us? How are we to feed our poor children, when we no longer have anything even for ourselves?'

'I'll tell you what, husband,' answered the woman, 'early tomorrow morning we will take the children out into the forest to where it is the thickest; there we will light a fire for them, and give each of them one more piece of bread, and then we will go to our work and leave them alone. They will not find the way home again, and we shall be rid of them.'

'No, wife,' said the man, 'I will not do that; how can I bear to leave my children alone in the forest? – the wild animals would soon come and tear them to pieces.'

'O, you fool!' said she, 'then we must all four die of hunger, you may as well plane the planks for our coffins,' and she left him no peace until he consented.

'But I feel very sorry for the poor children, all the same,' said the man.

The two children had also not been able to sleep for hunger, and had heard what their stepmother had said to their father. Gretel wept bitter tears, and said to Hansel: 'Now all is over with us.'

'Be quiet, Gretel,' said Hansel, 'do not distress yourself, I will soon find a way to help us.' And when the old folks had fallen asleep, he got up, put on his little coat, opened the door below, and crept outside. The moon shone brightly, and the white pebbles which lay in front of the house glittered like real silver pennies. Hansel stooped and stuffed the little pocket of his coat with as many as he could get in. Then he went back and said to Gretel: 'Be comforted, dear little sister, and sleep in peace, God will not forsake us,' and he lay down again in his bed.

When day dawned, but before the sun had risen, the woman came and awoke the two children, saying: 'Get up, you sluggards! we are going into the forest to fetch wood.' She gave each a little piece of bread, and said: 'There is something for your dinner, but do not eat it up before then, for you will get nothing else.'

Gretel took the bread under her apron, as Hansel had the pebbles in his pocket. Then they all set out together on the way to the forest. When they had walked a short time, Hansel stood still and peeped back at the house, and did so again and again.

His father said: 'Hansel, what are you looking at there and staying behind for? Pay attention, and do not forget how to use your legs.'

'Ah, father,' said Hansel, 'I am looking at my little white cat, which is sitting up on the roof, and wants to say goodbye to me.'

The wife said: 'Fool, that is not your little cat, that is the morning sun which is shining on the chimneys.'

Hansel, however, had not been looking back at the cat, but had been constantly throwing one of the white pebble-stones out of his pocket on the road.

When they had reached the middle of the forest, the father said: 'Now, children, pile up some wood, and
I will light a fire that you may not be cold.'
Hansel and Gretel gathered brushwood
together, as high as a little hill. The
brushwood was

Hansel had been constantly throwing the white pebble-stones.

lighted, and when the flames were burning
very high, the woman said: 'Now, children, lay
yourselves down by the fire and rest, we will go into the forest and cut some wood. When we have done, we will come back and fetch you away.'

Hansel and Gretel sat by the fire, and when noon came, each ate a little piece of bread, and as they heard the strokes of the wood-axe they believed that their father was near. It was not the axe, however, but a branch which he had fastened to a withered tree which the wind was blowing backwards and forwards. And as they had been sitting such a long time, their eyes closed with fatigue, and they fell fast asleep. When at last they awoke, it was already dark night. Gretel began to cry and said: 'How are we to get out of the forest now?'

But Hansel comforted her and said: 'Just wait a little, until the moon has risen, and then we will soon find the way.' And when the full moon had risen, Hansel took his little sister by the hand, and followed the pebbles which shone like newly-coined silver pieces, and showed them the way.

They walked the whole night long, and by break of day came once more to their father's house. They knocked at the door, and when the woman opened it and saw that it was Hansel and Gretel, she said: 'You naughty children, why have you slept so long in the forest? – we thought you were never coming back at all!' The father, however, rejoiced, for it had cut him to the heart to leave them behind alone.

Not long afterwards, there was once more great dearth throughout the land, and the children heard their mother saying at night to their father: 'Everything is eaten again, we have one half loaf left, and that is the end. The children must go, we will take them farther into the wood, so that they will not find their way out again; there is no other means of saving ourselves!'

The man's heart was heavy, and he thought: 'It would be better for you to share the last mouthful with your children.'

The woman, however, would listen to nothing that he had to say, but scolded and reproached him. He who says A must say B, likewise, and as he had yielded the first time, he had to do so a second time also.

The children, however, were still awake and had heard the conversation. When the old folks were asleep, Hansel again got up, and wanted to go out and pick up pebbles as he had done before, but the woman had locked the door, and Hansel could not get out. Nevertheless he comforted his little sister, and said: 'Do not cry, Gretel, go to sleep quietly, the good God will help us.'

Early in the morning came the woman, and took the children out of their beds. Their piece of bread was given to them, but it was still smaller than the time before. On the way into the forest Hansel crumbled his in his pocket, and often stood still and threw a morsel on the ground. 'Hansel, why do you stop and look round?' said the father, 'go on.'

'I am looking back at my little pigeon which is sitting on the roof, and wants to say goodbye to me,' answered Hansel.

'Fool!' said the woman, 'that is not your little pigeon, that is the morning sun that is shining on the chimney.'

Hansel, however little by little, threw all the crumbs on the path.

The woman led the children still deeper into the forest, where they had never in their lives been before. Then a great fire was again made, and the mother said: 'Just sit there, you children, and when you are tired you may sleep a little; we are going into the forest to cut wood, and in the evening when we are done, we will come and fetch you away.'

When it was noon, Gretel shared her piece of bread with Hansel, who had scattered his by the way. Then they fell asleep and evening passed, but no one came to the poor children. They did not awake until it was dark night, and Hansel comforted his little sister and said: 'Just wait, Gretel, until the moon rises, and then we shall see the crumbs of bread which I have strewn about, they will show us our way home again.' When the moon came they set out, but they found no crumbs, for the many thousands of birds which fly about in the woods and fields had picked them all up. Hansel said to Gretel: 'We shall soon find the way,' but they did not find it. They walked the whole night and all the next day too from morning till evening, but they did not get out of the forest, and were very hungry, for they had nothing to eat but two or three berries, which grew on the ground. And as they were so weary that their legs would carry them no longer, they lay down beneath a tree and fell asleep.

It was now three mornings since they had left their father's house. They began to walk again, but they always came deeper into the forest, and if help did not come soon, they must die of hunger and weariness. When it was mid-day, they saw a beautiful snow-white bird sitting on a bough, which sang so delightfully that they stood still and listened to it. And when its song was over, it spread its wings and flew away before them, and they followed it until they reached a little house, on the roof of which it alighted; and when they approached the little house they saw that it was built of bread and covered with cakes, but that the windows were of clear sugar. 'We will set to work on that,' said Hansel, 'and have a good meal. I will eat a bit of the roof, and you Gretel, can eat some of the window, it will taste sweet.' Hansel reached up above, and broke off a little of the roof to try how it tasted, and Gretel leant against the window and nibbled at the panes. Then a soft voice cried from the parlour:

'Nibble, nibble, gnaw,
    Who is nibbling at my little house?'

The children answered:

'The wind, the wind,
    The heaven-born wind,'

and went on eating without disturbing themselves. Hansel, who liked the taste of the roof, tore down a great piece of it, and Gretel pushed out the whole of one round window-pane, sat down, and enjoyed herself with it. Suddenly the door opened, and a woman as old as the hills, who supported herself

A woman came creeping out.

on crutches, came creeping out. Hansel and Gretel were so terribly frightened that they let fall what they had in their hands. The old woman, however, nodded her head, and said: 'Oh, you dear children, who has brought you here? do come in, and stay with me. No harm shall happen to you.' She took them both by the hand, and led them into her little house. Then good food was set before them, milk and pancakes, with sugar, apples, and nuts. Afterwards two pretty little beds were covered with clean white linen, and Hansel and Gretel lay down in them, and thought they were in heaven.

The old woman had only pretended to be so kind; she was in reality a wicked witch, who lay in wait for children, and had only built the little house of bread in order to entice them there. When a child fell into her power, she killed it, cooked and ate it, and that was a feast day with her. Witches have red eyes, and cannot see far, but they have a keen scent like the beasts, and are aware when human beings draw near. When

Hansel and Gretel came into her neighbourhood, she laughed with malice, and said mockingly: 'I have them, they shall not escape me again!' Early in the morning before the children were awake, she was already up, and when she saw both of them sleeping and looking so pretty, with their plump and rosy cheeks she muttered to herself: 'That will be a dainty mouthful!' Then she seized Hansel with her shrivelled hand, carried him into a little stable, and locked him in behind a grated door. Scream as he might, it would not help him. Then she went to Gretel, shook her till she awoke, and cried: 'Get up, lazy thing, fetch some water, and cook something good for your brother, he is in the stable outside, and is to be made fat. When he is fat, I will eat him.' Gretel began to weep bitterly, but it was all in vain, for she was forced to do what the wicked witch commanded.

And now the best food was cooked for poor Hansel, but Gretel got nothing but crab-shells. Every morning the woman crept to the little stable, and cried: 'Hansel, stretch out your finger that I may feel if you will soon be fat.' Hansel, however, stretched out a little bone to her, and the old woman, who had dim eyes, could not see it, and thought it was Hansel's finger, and was astonished that there was no way of fattening him. When four weeks had gone by, and Hansel still remained thin, she was seized with impatience and would not wait any longer. 'Now, then, Gretel,' she cried to the girl, 'stir yourself, and bring some water. Let Hansel be fat or lean, tomorrow I will kill him, and cook him.'

Ah, how the poor little sister did lament when she had to fetch the water, and how her tears did flow down her cheeks! 'Dear God, do help us,' she cried. 'If the wild beasts in the forest had but devoured us, we should at any rate have died together.'

'Just keep your noise to yourself,' said the old woman, 'it won't help you at all.'

Early in the morning, Gretel had to go out and hang
up the cauldron with the water, and light the fire.
'We will bake first,' said the old woman, 'I have
already heated the oven, and kneaded the
dough.' She pushed poor Gretel out to
the oven, from which flames of fire
were already darting. 'Creep
in,' said the witch, 'and see
if it is properly heated,
so that we can put
the bread in.'

And once

'Hansel, stretch out your
finger that I may feel if
you will soon be fat.'

Gretel was inside, she
intended to shut the oven and let her
bake in it, and then she would eat her, too.

But Gretel saw what she had in mind, and said: 'I do not
know how I am to do it; how do I get in?'

'Silly goose,' said the old woman. 'The door is big enough;
just look, I can get in myself!' and she crept up and thrust her
head into the oven. Then Gretel gave her a push that drove her
far into it, and shut the iron door, and fastened the bolt. Oh!
then she began to howl quite horribly, but Gretel ran away
and the godless witch was miserably burnt to death.

Gretel, however, ran like lightning to Hansel, opened his
little stable, and cried: 'Hansel, we are saved! The old witch

Gretel gave her a push.

is dead!' Then Hansel sprang like a bird from its cage when the door is opened. How they did rejoice and embrace each other, and dance about and kiss each other! And as they had no longer any need to fear her, they went into the witch's house, and in every corner there stood chests full of pearls and jewels. 'These are far better than pebbles!' said Hansel, and thrust into his pockets whatever could be got in, and Gretel said: 'I, too, will take something home with me,' and filled her pinafore full.

'But now we must be off,' said Hansel, 'that we may get out of the witch's forest.'

When they had walked for two hours, they came to a great stretch of water. 'We cannot cross,' said Hansel, 'I see no foot-plank, and no bridge.'

'And there is also no ferry,' answered Gretel, 'but a white duck is swimming there: if I ask her, she will help us over.' Then she cried:

'Little duck, little duck, dost thou see,
Hansel and Gretel are waiting for thee?
There's never a plank, or bridge in sight,
Take us across on thy back so white.'

The duck came to them, and Hansel seated himself on its back, and told his sister to sit by him.

'No,' replied Gretel, 'that will be too heavy for the little duck; she shall take us across, one after the other.' The good little duck did so, and when they were once safely across and had walked for a short time, the forest seemed to be more and more familiar to them, and at length they saw from afar their father's house. Then they began to run, rushed into the parlour, and threw themselves round their father's neck. The man had not known one happy hour since he had left the children in the forest; the woman, however, was dead. Gretel emptied her pinafore until pearls and precious stones ran about the room, and Hansel threw one handful after another out of his pocket to add to them. Then all anxiety was at an end, and they lived together in perfect happiness.

7

The Frog Prince

One fine evening a young princess put on her bonnet and clogs, and went out to take a walk by herself in a wood; and when she came to a cool spring of water, that rose in the midst of it, she sat herself down to rest a while. Now she had a golden ball in her hand, which was her favourite plaything; and she was always tossing it up into the air, and catching it again as it fell. After a time she threw it up so high that she missed catching it as it fell; and the ball bounded away, and rolled along upon the ground, till at last it fell down into the spring. The princess looked into the spring after her ball, but it was very deep, so deep that she could not see the bottom of it. Then she began to bewail her loss, and said, 'Alas! if I could only get my ball again, I would give all my fine clothes and jewels, and everything that I have in the world.'

Whilst she was speaking, a frog put its head out of the water, and said, 'Princess, why do you weep so bitterly?'

'Alas!' said she, 'what can you do for me, you nasty frog? My golden ball has fallen into the spring.'

The frog said, 'I want not your pearls, and jewels, and fine clothes; but if you will love me, and let me live with you and eat from off your golden plate, and sleep upon your bed, I will bring you your ball again.'

'What nonsense,' thought the princess, 'this silly frog is talking! He can never even get out of the spring to visit me, though he may be able to get my ball for me, and therefore I will tell him he shall have what he asks.' So she said to the frog, 'Well, if you will bring me my ball, I will do all you ask.' Then the frog put his head down, and dived deep under the water; and after a little while he came up again, with the ball in his mouth, and threw it on the edge of the spring.

As soon as the young princess saw her ball, she ran to pick it up; and she was so overjoyed to have it in her hand again, that she never thought of the frog, but ran home with it as fast as she could.

The frog called after her, 'Stay, princess, and take me with you as you said,' but she did not stop to hear a word.

A frog put its head out of the water.

The next day, just as the princess had sat down to dinner, she heard a strange noise – tap, tap – plash, plash – as if something was coming up the marble staircase: and soon afterwards there was a gentle knock at the door, and a little voice cried out and said:

'Open the door, my princess dear,
Open the door to thy true love here!
And mind the words that thou and I said
By the fountain cool, in the greenwood shade.'

Then the princess ran to the door and opened it, and there she saw the frog, whom she had quite forgotten. At this sight she was sadly frightened, and shutting the door as fast as she could came back to her seat. The king, her father, seeing that something had frightened her, asked her what was the matter. 'There is a nasty frog,' said she, 'at the door, that lifted my ball for me out of the spring this morning: I told him that he should live with me here, thinking that he could never get out of the spring; but there he is at the door, and he wants to come in.' While she was speaking the frog knocked again at the door, and said:

'Open the door, my princess dear,
Open the door to thy true love here!
And mind the words that thou and I said
By the fountain cool, in the greenwood shade.'

Then the king said to the young princess, 'As you have given your word you must keep it; so go and let him in.' She did so, and the frog hopped into the room, and then straight on – tap, tap – plash, plash – from the bottom of the room to the top, till he came up close to the table where the princess sat.

'Pray lift me upon chair,' said he to the princess, 'and let me sit next to you.'

As soon as she had done this, the frog said, 'Put your plate nearer to me, that I may eat out of it.'

She put him upon the pillow of her own bed.

This she did, and when he had eaten as much as he could, he said, 'Now I am tired; carry me upstairs, and put me into your bed.' And the princess, though very unwilling, took him up in her hand, and put him upon the pillow of her own bed, where he slept all night long. As soon as it was light he jumped up, hopped downstairs, and went out of the house.

'Now, then,' thought the princess, 'at last he is gone, and I shall be troubled with him no more.'

But she was mistaken; for when night came again she heard the same tapping at the door; and the frog came once more, and said:

'Open the door, my princess dear,
Open the door to thy true love here!
And mind the words that thou and I said
By the fountain cool, in the greenwood shade.'

And when the princess opened the door the frog came in, and slept upon her pillow as before, till the morning broke. And the third night he did the same. But when the princess awoke on the following morning she was astonished to see, instead of the frog, a handsome prince, gazing on her with the most beautiful eyes she had ever seen, and standing at the head of her bed.

He told her that he had been enchanted by a spiteful fairy, who had changed him into a frog; and that he had been fated so to abide till some princess should take him out of the spring, and let him eat from her plate, and sleep upon her bed for three nights. 'You,' said the prince, 'have broken his cruel charm, and now I have nothing to wish for but that you should go with me into my father's kingdom, where I will marry you, and love you as long as you live.'

The young princess, you may be sure, was not long in saying 'Yes' to all this; and as they spoke a gay coach drove up, with eight beautiful horses, decked with plumes of feathers and a golden harness; and behind the coach rode the prince's servant, faithful Heinrich, who had bewailed the misfortunes of his dear master during his enchantment so long and so bitterly, that his heart had well-nigh burst.

They then took leave of the king, and got into the coach with eight horses, and all set out, full of joy and merriment, for the prince's kingdom, which they reached safely; and there they lived happily a great many years.

8

Rapunzel

There were once a man and a woman who had long in vain wished for a child. At length the woman hoped that God was about to grant her desire. These people had a little window at the back of their house from which a splendid garden could be seen, which was full of the most beautiful flowers and herbs. It was, however, surrounded by a high wall, and no one dared to go into it because it belonged to an enchantress, who had great power and was dreaded by all the world. One day the woman was standing by this window and looking down into the garden, when she saw a bed which was planted with the most beautiful rampion (rapunzel), and it looked so fresh and green that she longed for it, she quite pined away, and began to look pale and miserable.

Then her husband was alarmed, and asked: 'What ails you, dear wife?'

'Ah,' she replied, 'if I can't eat some of the rampion, which is in the garden behind our house, I shall die.'

The man, who loved her, thought: 'Sooner than let your wife die, bring her some of the rampion yourself, let it cost what it will.' At twilight, he clambered down over the wall into the garden of the enchantress, hastily clutched a handful of rampion, and took it to his wife.

She at once made herself a salad of it, and ate it greedily. It tasted so good to her – so very good, that the next day she longed for it three times as much as before. If he was to have any rest, her husband must once more descend into the garden. In the gloom of evening therefore, he let himself down again; but when he had clambered down the wall he was terribly afraid, for he saw the enchantress standing before him.

'How can you dare,' said she with angry look, 'descend into my garden and steal my rampion like a thief? You shall suffer for it!'

'Ah,' answered he, 'let mercy take the place of justice, I only made up my mind to do it out of necessity. My wife saw your rampion from the window, and felt such a longing for it that she would have died if she had not got some to eat.'

Then the enchantress allowed her anger to be softened, and said to him: 'If the case be as you say, I will allow you to take away with you as much rampion as you will, only I make one

He saw the enchantress standing before him.

condition, you must give me the child which your wife will bring into the world; it shall be well treated, and I will care for it like a mother.'

The man in his terror consented to everything, and when the woman was brought to bed, the enchantress appeared at once, gave the child the name of Rapunzel, and took it away with her.

Rapunzel grew into the most beautiful child under the sun. When she was twelve years old, the enchantress shut her into a tower, which lay in a forest, and had neither stairs nor door, but quite at the top was a little window. When the enchantress wanted to go in, she placed herself beneath it and cried:

'Rapunzel, Rapunzel,
Let down your hair to me.'

Rapunzel had magnificent long hair, fine as spun gold, and when she heard the voice of the enchantress she unfastened her braided tresses, wound them round one of the hooks of the window above, and then the hair fell twenty ells down, and the enchantress climbed up by it.

After a year or two, it came to pass that the king's son rode through the forest and passed by the tower. Then he heard a song, which was so charming that he stood still and listened. This was Rapunzel, who in her solitude passed her time in letting her sweet voice resound. The king's son wanted to climb up to her, and looked for the door of the tower, but none was to be found. He rode home, but the singing had so deeply touched his heart, that every day he went out into the forest and listened to it. Once when he was thus standing behind a tree, he saw that an enchantress came there, and he heard how she cried:

'Rapunzel, Rapunzel,
Let down your hair to me.'

Then Rapunzel let down the
braids of her hair, and the
enchantress climbed up to
her. 'If that is the ladder by
which one mounts, I too will
try my fortune,' said he, and
the next day when it began to
grow dark, he went to the tower
and cried:

'Rapunzel, Rapunzel,
Let down your hair to me.'

Immediately the hair fell
down and the king's son
climbed up.

At first Rapunzel was terribly
frightened when a man, such as her
eyes had never yet beheld, came to
her; but the king's son began to
talk to her quite like a friend,
and told her that his heart
had been so stirred that it had
let him have no rest, and he
had been forced to see her.

Then Rapunzel lost her fear, and
when he asked her if she would
take him for her husband, and
she saw that he was young and
handsome, she thought: 'He

The king's son climbed up.

will love me more than old Dame Gothel does'; and she said yes, and laid her hand in his. She said: 'I will willingly go away with you, but I do not know how to get down. Bring with you a skein of silk every time that you come, and I will weave a ladder with it, and when that is ready I will descend, and you will take me on your horse.'

They agreed that until that time he should come to her every evening, for the old woman came by day. The enchantress remarked nothing of this, until once Rapunzel said to her: 'Tell me, Dame Gothel, how it happens that you are so much heavier for me to draw up than the young king's son – he is with me in a moment.'

'Ah! you wicked child,' cried the enchantress. 'What do I hear you say! I thought I had separated you from all the world, and yet you have deceived me!' In her anger she clutched Rapunzel's beautiful tresses, wrapped them twice round her left hand, seized a pair of scissors with the right, and snip, snap, they were cut off, and the lovely braids lay on the ground. And she was so pitiless that she took poor Rapunzel into a desert where she had to live in great grief and misery.

On the same day that she cast out Rapunzel, however, the enchantress fastened the braids of hair, which she had cut off, to the hook of the window, and when the king's son came and cried:

'Rapunzel, Rapunzel,
Let down your hair to me.'

She let the hair down. The king's son ascended, but instead of finding his dearest Rapunzel, he found the enchantress, who gazed at him with wicked and venomous looks.

'Aha!' she cried mockingly, 'you would fetch your dearest, but the beautiful bird sits no longer singing in the nest; the cat has got it, and will scratch out your eyes as well. Rapunzel is lost to you; you will never see her again.'

The king's son was beside himself with pain, and in his despair he leapt down from the tower. He escaped with his life, but the thorns into which he fell pierced his eyes. Then he wandered quite blind about the forest, ate nothing but roots and berries, and did naught but lament and weep over the loss of his dearest wife. Thus he roamed about in misery for some years, and at length came to the desert where Rapunzel, with the twins to which she had given birth, a boy and a girl, lived in wretchedness. He heard a voice, and it seemed so familiar to him that he went towards it, and when he approached, Rapunzel knew him and fell on his neck and wept. Two of her tears wetted his eyes and they grew clear again, and he could see with them as before. He led her to his kingdom where he was joyfully received, and they lived for a long time afterwards, happy and contented.

9

Little Red Riding Hood

Once upon a time there was a dear little girl who was loved by everyone who looked at her, but most of all by her grandmother, and there was nothing that she would not have given to the child. Once she gave her a little cap of red velvet, which suited her so well that she would never wear anything else; so she was always called 'Little Red-Cap.'

One day her mother said to her: 'Come, Little Red-Cap, here is a piece of cake and a bottle of wine; take them to your grandmother, she is ill and weak, and they will do her good. Set out before it gets hot, and when you are going, walk nicely and quietly and do not run off the path, or you may fall and break the bottle, and then your grandmother will get nothing; and when you go into her room, don't forget to say, "Good morning", and don't peep into every corner before you do it.'

'I will take great care,' said Little Red-Cap to her mother, and gave her hand on it.

The grandmother lived out in the wood, half a league from the village, and just as Little Red-Cap entered the wood, a wolf met her. Red-Cap did not know what a wicked creature he was, and was not at all afraid of him.

'Good day, Little Red-Cap,' said he.

'Thank you kindly, wolf.'

'Whither away so early, Little Red-Cap?'

'To my grandmother's.'

'What have you got in your apron?'

'Cake and wine; yesterday was baking-day, so poor sick grandmother is to have something good, to make her stronger.'

'Where does your grandmother live, Little Red-Cap?'

'A good quarter of a league farther on in the wood; her house stands under the three large oak-trees, the nut-trees are just below; you surely must know it,' replied Little Red-Cap.

The wolf thought to himself: 'What a tender young creature! what a nice plump mouthful – she will be better to eat than the old woman. I must act craftily, so as to catch both.' So he walked for a short time by the side of Little Red-Cap, and then he said: 'See, Little Red-Cap, how pretty the flowers are about here – why do you not look round? I believe, too, that you do not hear how sweetly the little birds are singing; you walk gravely along as if you were going to school, while everything else out here in the wood is merry.'

Little Red-Cap raised her eyes, and when she saw the sunbeams dancing here and there through the trees, and pretty flowers growing everywhere, she thought: 'Suppose I take grandmother a fresh nosegay; that would please her too. It is so early in the day that I shall still get there in good time'; and so she ran from the path into the wood to look for flowers. And whenever she had picked one, she fancied that she saw a still prettier one farther on, and ran after it, and so got deeper and deeper into the wood.

Meanwhile the wolf ran straight to the grandmother's house and knocked at the door.

'Who is there?'

'Little Red-Cap,' replied the wolf. 'She is bringing cake and wine; open the door.'

'Lift the latch,' called out the grandmother, 'I am too weak, and cannot get up.'

The wolf lifted the latch, the door sprang open, and without saying a word he went straight to the grandmother's bed, and devoured her. Then he put on her clothes, dressed himself in her cap, laid himself in bed and drew the curtains.

He put on her clothes, dressed himself in her cap, laid himself in bed and drew the curtains.

Little Red-Cap, however, had been running about picking flowers, and when she had gathered so many that she could carry no more, she remembered her grandmother, and set out on the way to her.

She was surprised to find the cottage-door standing open, and when she went into the room, she had such a strange feeling that she said to herself: 'Oh dear! how uneasy I feel today, and at other times I like being with grandmother so much.' She called out: 'Good morning,' but received no answer;

so she went to the bed and drew back the curtains. There lay her grandmother with her cap pulled far over her face, and looking very strange.

'Oh! grandmother,' she said, 'what big ears you have!'

'The better to hear you with, my child,' was the reply.

'But, grandmother, what big eyes you have!' she said.

'The better to see you with, my dear.'

'But, grandmother, what large hands you have!'

'The better to hug you with.'

'Oh! but, grandmother, what a terrible big mouth you have!'

'The better to eat you with!'

And scarcely had the wolf said this, than with one bound he was out of bed and swallowed up Red-Cap.

When the wolf had appeased his appetite, he lay down again in the bed, fell asleep and began to snore very loud.

The huntsman was just passing the house, and thought to himself: 'How the old woman is snoring! I must just see if she wants anything.' So he went into the room, and when he came to the bed, he saw that the wolf was lying in it. 'Do I find you here, you old sinner!' said he. 'I have long sought you!' Then just as he was going to fire at him, it occurred to him that the wolf might have devoured the grandmother, and that she might still be saved, so he did not fire, but took a pair of scissors, and began to cut open the stomach of the sleeping wolf.

When he had made two snips, he saw the little Red-Cap shining, and then he made two snips more, and the little girl sprang out, crying: 'Ah, how frightened I have been! How dark it was inside the wolf'; and after that the aged grandmother came out alive also, but scarcely able to breathe. Red-Cap, however, quickly fetched great stones with which they filled the wolf's belly, and when he awoke, he wanted to run away, but the stones were so heavy that he collapsed at once, and fell dead.

Then all three were delighted. The huntsman drew off the wolf's skin and went home with it; the grandmother ate the cake and drank the wine which Red-Cap had brought, and revived, but Red-Cap thought to herself: 'As long as I live, I will never by myself leave the path, to run into the wood, when my mother has forbidden me to do so.'

It also related that once when Red-Cap was again taking cakes to the old grandmother, another wolf spoke to her, and tried to entice her from the path. Red-Cap, however, was on her guard, and went straight forward on her way, and told her grandmother that she had met the wolf, and that he had said 'good morning' to her, but with such a wicked look in his eyes, that if they had not been on the public road she was certain he would have eaten her up. 'Well,' said the grandmother, 'we will shut the door, that he may not come in.'

Soon afterwards the wolf knocked, and cried: 'Open the door, grandmother, I am Little Red-Cap, and am bringing you some cakes.' But they did not speak, or open the door, so the grey-beard stole twice or thrice round the house, and at last jumped on the roof, intending to wait until Red-Cap went home in the evening, and then to steal after her and devour her in the darkness.

But the grandmother saw what was in his thoughts. In front of the house was a great stone trough, so she said to the child: 'Take the pail, Red-Cap; I made some sausages yesterday, so carry the water in which I boiled them to the trough.' Red-Cap carried until the great trough was quite full. Then the smell of the sausages reached the wolf, and he sniffed and peeped down, and at last stretched out his neck so far that he could no longer keep his footing and began to slip, and slipped down from the roof straight into the great trough, and was drowned. But Red-Cap went joyously home, and no one ever did anything to harm her again.

10

Rumpelstiltskin

y the side of a wood, in a country a long way off, ran a fine stream of water; and upon the stream there stood a mill. The miller's house was close by, and the miller, you must know, had a very beautiful daughter. She was, moreover, very shrewd and clever; and the miller was so proud of her, that he one day told the king of the land, who used to come and hunt in the wood, that his daughter could spin gold out of straw. Now this king was very fond of money; and when he heard the miller's boast his greediness was raised, and he sent for the girl to be brought before him. Then he led her to a chamber in his palace where there was a great heap of straw, and gave her a spinning-wheel, and said, 'All this must be spun into gold before morning, as you love your life.' It was in vain that the poor maiden said that it was only a silly boast of her father, for that she could do no such thing as spin straw into gold: the chamber door was locked, and she was left alone.

She sat down in one corner of the room, and began to bewail her hard fate; when on a sudden the door opened, and a droll-looking little man hobbled in, and said, 'Good morrow to you, my good lass; what are you weeping for?'

'Alas!' said she, 'I must spin this straw into gold, and I know not how.'

'What will you give me,' said the hobgoblin, 'to do it for you?'

'My necklace,' replied the maiden.

He took her at her word, and sat himself down to the wheel, and whistled and sang:

'Round about, round about,
Lo and behold!
Reel away, reel away,
Straw into gold!'

And round about
the wheel went
merrily; the
work   was
quickly done,
and the straw
was all spun
into gold.
    When the
king came
and saw this,
he was greatly
astonished and
pleased; but his
heart grew still more
greedy of gain, and he
shut up the poor miller's
daughter again with a fresh
task. Then she knew not what to do,
and sat down once more to weep; but the dwarf soon opened
the door, and said, 'What will you give me to do your task?'

The straw was all
spun into gold.

'The ring on my finger,' said she.

So her little friend took the ring, and began to work at the wheel again, and whistled and sang:

'Round about, round about,
Lo and behold!
Reel away, reel away,
Straw into gold!'

Till, long before morning, all was done again.

The king was greatly delighted to see all this glittering treasure; but still he had not enough: so he took the miller's daughter to a yet larger heap, and said, 'All this must be spun tonight; and if it is, you shall be my queen.'

As soon as she was alone that dwarf came in, and said, 'What will you give me to spin gold for you this third time?'

'I have nothing left,' said she.

'Then say you will give me,' said the little man, 'the first little child that you may have when you are queen.'

'That may never be,' thought the miller's daughter: and as she knew no other way to get her task done, she said she would do what he asked. Round went the wheel again to the old song, and the manikin once more spun the heap into gold. The king came in the morning, and, finding all he wanted, was forced to keep his word; so he married the miller's daughter, and she really became queen.

At the birth of her first little child she was very glad, and forgot the dwarf, and what she had said. But one day he came into her room, where she was sitting playing with her baby, and put her in mind of it. Then she grieved sorely at her misfortune, and said she would give him all the wealth of the kingdom if he would let her off, but in vain; till at last her tears softened him, and he said, 'I will give you three days' grace, and if during that time you tell me my name, you shall keep your child.'

Now the queen lay awake all night, thinking of all the odd names that she had ever heard; and she sent messengers all over the land to find out new ones. The next day the little man came, and she began with TIMOTHY, ICHABOD, BENJAMIN, JEREMIAH, and all the names she could remember; but to all and each of them he said, 'Madam, that is not my name.'

The second day she began with all the comical names she could hear of, BANDY-LEGS, HUNCHBACK, CROOK-SHANKS, and so on; but the little gentleman still said to every one of them, 'Madam, that is not my name.'

The third day one of the messengers came back, and said, 'I have travelled two days without hearing of any other names; but yesterday, as I was climbing a high hill, among the trees of the forest where the fox and the hare bid each other good night, I saw a little hut; and before the hut burnt a fire; and round about the fire a funny little dwarf was dancing upon one leg, and singing:

'Merrily the feast I'll make.
Today I'll brew, tomorrow bake;
Merrily I'll dance and sing,
For next day will a stranger bring.
Little does my lady dream
Rumpelstiltskin is my name!'

When the queen heard this she jumped for joy, and as soon as her little friend came she sat down upon her throne, and called all her court round to enjoy the fun; and the nurse stood by her side with the baby in her arms, as if it was quite ready to be given up.

Then the little man began to chuckle at the thought of having the poor child, to take home with him to his hut in the woods; and he cried out, 'Now, lady, what is my name?'

'Is it JOHN?' asked she.

'No, madam!'

'Is it TOM?'

'No, madam!'

'Is it JEMMY?'

'It is not.'

'Can your name be RUMPELSTILTSKIN?' said the lady slyly.

'Some witch told you that! – some witch told you that!' cried the little man, and dashed his right foot in a rage so deep into the floor, that he was forced to lay hold of it with both hands to pull it out.

Then he made the best of his way off, while the nurse laughed and the baby crowed; and all the court jeered at him for having had so much trouble for nothing, and said, 'We wish you a very good morning, and a merry feast, Mr RUMPELSTILTSKIN!

He dashed his right foot deep into the floor.

11

Jack and the Beanstalk

There was once upon a time a poor widow who had an only son named Jack, and a cow named Milky-white. And all they had to live on was the milk the cow gave every morning which they carried to the market and sold. But one morning Milky-white gave no milk and they didn't know what to do.

'What shall we do, what shall we do?' said the widow, wringing her hands.

'Cheer up, mother, I'll go and get work somewhere,' said Jack.

'We've tried that before, and nobody would take you,' said his mother; 'we must sell Milky-white and with the money do something, start a shop, or something.'

'All right, mother,' says Jack; 'it's market-day today, and I'll soon sell Milky-white, and then we'll see what we can do.'

So he took the cow's halter in his hand, and off he starts. He hadn't gone far when he met a funny-looking old man who said to him: 'Good morning, Jack.'

'Good morning to you,' said Jack, and wondered how he knew his name.

'Well, Jack, and where are you off to?' said the man.

'I'm going to market to sell our cow here.'

'Oh, you look the proper sort of chap to sell cows,' said the man; 'I wonder if you know how many beans make five.'

'Two in each hand and one in your mouth,' says Jack, as sharp as a needle.

'Right you are,' said the man, 'and here they are the very beans themselves,' he went on pulling out of his pocket a number of strange-looking beans. 'As you are so sharp,' says he, 'I don't mind doing a swop with you – your cow for these beans.'

'Walker!' says Jack; 'wouldn't you like it?'

'Ah! you don't know what these beans are,' said the man; 'if you plant them over-night, by morning they grow right up to the sky.'

'Really?' says Jack; 'you don't say so.'

'Yes, that is so, and if it doesn't turn out to be true you can have your cow back.'

'Right,' says Jack, and hands him over Milky-white's halter and pockets the beans.

Back goes Jack home, and as he hadn't gone very far it wasn't dusk by the time he got to his door.

'What back, Jack?' said his mother; 'I see you haven't got Milky-white, so you've sold her. How much did you get for her?'

'You'll never guess, mother,' says Jack.

'No, you don't say so. Good boy! Five pounds, ten, fifteen, no, it can't be twenty.'

'I told you you couldn't guess, what do you say to these beans; they're magical, plant them over-night and –'

'What!' says Jack's mother, 'have you been such a fool, such a dolt, such an idiot, as to give away my Milky-white, the best milker in the parish, and prime beef to boot, for a set of paltry beans. Take that! Take that! Take that! And as for your precious beans here they go out of the window. And now

off with you to bed. Not
a sup shall you drink, and
not a bit shall you swallow
this very night.'

So Jack went upstairs
to his little room in the
attic, and sad and sorry
he was, to be sure, as much
for his mother's sake, as for
the loss of his supper.

At last he dropped
off to sleep.

When he woke
up, the room looked
so funny. The sun was
shining into part of it, and
yet all the rest was quite dark
and shady. So Jack jumped
up and dressed himself and
went to the window.
And what do you think
he saw? why, the beans
his mother had thrown
out of the window into
the garden, had sprung up
into a big beanstalk which
went up and up and up
till it reached the sky.
So the man spoke truth
after all.

The beanstalk grew up
quite close past Jack's
window, so all he had to

Jack climbed
and he climbed.

do was to open it and give a jump on to the beanstalk which was made like a big plaited ladder. So Jack climbed and he climbed and he climbed and he climbed and he climbed and he climbed and he climbed till at last he reached the sky. And when he got there he found a long broad road going as straight as a dart. So he walked along and he walked along and he walked along till he came to a great big tall house, and on the doorstep there was a great big tall woman.

'Good morning, mum,' says Jack, quite polite-like. 'Could you be so kind as to give me some breakfast.' For he hadn't had anything to eat, you know, the night before and was as hungry as a hunter.

'It's breakfast you want, is it?' says the great big tall woman, 'it's breakfast you'll be if you don't move off from here. My man is an ogre and there's nothing he likes better than boys broiled on toast. You'd better be moving on or he'll soon be coming.'

'Oh! please mum, do give me something to eat, mum. I've had nothing to eat since yesterday morning, really and truly, mum,' says Jack. 'I may as well be broiled, as die of hunger.'

Well, the ogre's wife wasn't such a bad sort, after all. So she took Jack into the kitchen, and gave him a junk of bread and cheese and a jug of milk. But Jack hadn't half finished these when thump! thump! thump! the whole house began to tremble with the noise of someone coming.

'Goodness gracious me! It's my old man,' said the ogre's wife, 'what on earth shall I do? Here, come quick and jump in here.' And she bundled Jack into the oven just as the ogre came in.

He was a big one, to be sure. At his belt he had three calves strung up by the heels, and he unhooked them and threw them down on the table and said: 'Here, wife, broil me a couple of these for breakfast. Ah what's this I smell?

Fee-fi-fo-fum,
I smell the blood of an Englishman,
Be he alive, or be he dead
I'll have his bones to grind my bread.

'Fee-fi-fo-fum, I smell the blood of an Englishman!'

'Nonsense, dear,' said his wife, 'you're dreaming. Or perhaps you smell the scraps of that little boy you liked so much for yesterday's dinner. Here, go you and have a wash and tidy up, and by the time you come back your breakfast'll be ready for you.'

So the ogre went off, and Jack was just going to jump out of the oven and run off when the woman told him not. 'Wait till he's asleep,' says she; 'he always has a snooze after breakfast.'

Well, the ogre had his breakfast, and after that he goes to a big chest and takes out of it a couple of bags of gold and sits down counting them till at last his head began to nod and he began to snore till the whole house shook again.

Then Jack crept out on tiptoe from his oven, and as he was passing the ogre he took one of the bags of gold under his arm, and off he pelters till he came to the beanstalk, and then he threw down the bag of gold which of course fell in to his mother's garden, and then he climbed down and climbed down till at last he got home and told his mother and showed her the gold and said: 'Well, mother, wasn't I right about the beans. They are really magical, you see.'

So they lived on the bag of gold for some time, but at last they came to the end of that so Jack made up his mind to try his luck once more up at the top of the beanstalk. So one fine morning he got up early, and got on to the beanstalk, and he climbed and he climbed and he climbed and he climbed and he climbed and he climbed till at last he got on the road again and came to the great big tall house he had been to before. There, sure enough, was the great big tall woman a-standing on the door-step.

'Good morning, mum,' says Jack, as bold as brass, 'could you be so good as to give me something to eat?'

'Go away, my boy,' said the big, tall woman, 'or else my man will eat you up for breakfast. But aren't you the youngster who came here once before? Do you know, that very day, my man missed one of his bags of gold.'

'That's strange, mum,' says Jack, 'I dare say I could tell you something about that but I'm so hungry I can't speak till I've had something to eat.'

Well the big tall woman was that curious that she took him in and gave him something to eat. But he had scarcely begun munching it as slowly as he could when thump! thump! thump! they heard the giant's footstep, and his wife hid Jack away in the oven.

All happened as it did before. In came the ogre as he did before, said: 'Fee-fi-fo-fum,' and had his breakfast off three broiled oxen. Then he said: 'Wife, bring me the hen that lays the golden eggs.' So she brought it, and the ogre said: 'Lay,' and it laid an egg all of gold. And then the ogre began to nod his head, and to snore till the house shook.

Then Jack crept out of the oven on tiptoe and caught hold of the golden hen, and was off before you could say 'Jack Robinson.' But this time the hen gave a cackle which woke the ogre, and just as Jack got out of the house he heard him calling: 'Wife, wife, what have you done with my golden hen?'

And the wife said: 'Why, my dear?'

But that was all Jack heard, for he rushed off to the beanstalk and climbed down like a house on fire. And when he got home he showed his mother the wonderful hen and said 'Lay,' to it; and it laid a golden egg every time he said 'Lay.'

Well, Jack was not content, and it wasn't very long before he determined to have another try at his luck up there at the top of the beanstalk. So one fine morning, he got up early, and went on to the beanstalk, and he climbed and he climbed and he climbed and he climbed till he got to the top. But this time he knew better than to go straight to the ogre's house. And when he got near it he waited behind a bush till he saw the ogre's wife come out with a pail to get some water, and then he crept into the house and got into the copper. He hadn't been there long when he heard thump! thump! thump! as before, and in come the ogre and his wife.

'Fee-fi-fo-fum, I smell the blood of an Englishman,' cried out the ogre; 'I smell him, wife, I smell him.'

'Do you, my dearie?' says the ogre's wife. 'Then if it's that little rogue that stole your gold and the hen that laid the golden eggs he's sure to have got into the oven.' And they both rushed to the oven. But Jack wasn't there, luckily, and the ogre's wife said: 'There you are again with your fee-fi-fo-fum. Why of course it's the laddie you caught last night that

I've broiled for your breakfast. How forgetful I am, and how careless you are not to tell the difference between a live un and a dead un.'

So the ogre sat down to the breakfast and ate it, but every now and then he would mutter: 'Well, I could have sworn –' and he'd get up and search the larder and the cupboards, and everything, only luckily he didn't think of the copper.

After breakfast was over, the ogre called out: 'Wife, wife, bring me my golden harp.' So she brought it and put it on the table before him. Then he said: 'Sing!' and the golden harp sang most beautifully. And it went on singing till the ogre fell asleep, and commenced to snore like thunder.

Then Jack lifted up the copper-lid very quietly and got down like a mouse and crept on hands and knees till he got to the table when he got up and caught hold of the golden harp and dashed with it towards the door. But the harp called out quite loud: 'Master! Master!' and the ogre woke up just in time to see Jack running off with his harp.

Jack ran as fast as he could, and the ogre came rushing after, and would soon have caught him only Jack had a start and dodged him a bit and knew where he was going. When he got to the beanstalk the ogre was not more than twenty yards away when suddenly he saw Jack disappear, and when he got up to the end of the road he saw Jack underneath climbing down for dear life. Well, the ogre didn't like trusting himself to such a ladder, and he stood and waited, so Jack got another start. But just then the harp cried out: 'Master! master!' and the ogre swung himself down on to the beanstalk which shook with his weight. Down climbs Jack, and after him climbed the ogre.

By this time Jack had climbed down and climbed down and climbed down till he was very nearly home. So he called out: 'Mother! mother! bring me an axe, bring me an axe.' And his mother came rushing out with the axe in her hand, but when

'Mother! mother! bring me an axe, bring me an axe.'

she came to the beanstalk she stood stock still with fright for there she saw the ogre just coming down below the clouds.

But Jack jumped down and got hold of the axe and gave a chop at the beanstalk which cut it half in two. The ogre felt the beanstalk shake and quiver so he stopped to see what was the matter. Then Jack gave another chop with the axe, and the beanstalk was cut in two and began to topple over. Then the ogre fell down and broke his crown, and the beanstalk came toppling after.

Then Jack showed his mother his golden harp, and what with showing that and selling the golden eggs, Jack and his mother became very rich, and he married a great princess, and they lived happy ever after.

Also available in this series

ILLUSTRATE
YOUR OWN

978 0 7509 9494 1

ILLUSTRATE
YOUR OWN

The
Wind in the
Willows

Kenneth Grahame

978 0 7509 9495 8

ILLUSTRATE
YOUR OWN

Alice's
Adventures in
Wonderland

Lewis Carroll

978 0 7509 9492 7

More from The History Press

978 0 7509 9012 7

COLOURING HISTORY

THE
TUDORS

NATALIE GRUENINGER
ILLUSTRATED BY KATHRYN HOLEMAN

978 0 7509 7944 3

The History Press

The destination for history
www.thehistorypress.co.uk